'Malcolm was about to turn sadly away when he noticed the waistcoat. The back was black silk, but the front was a shimmering mass of colour. It was a rainbow... you couldn't quite tell where one colour ended and the next began. He looked at the price—only £1.25.

Glowing with the thrill of a bargain, he took it to the counter. It was just the thing to make Helena notice him at the school disco.'

Finding the waistcoat is the first good thing to happen in ages. Life has been difficult since Dad lost his job. Can the boredom be about to end?

Plenty *is* about to happen, for the waistcoat holds a secret. As he daydreams, Malcolm fails to notice two dubious characters shadowing his every move...

Hilary Brand lives with her family in South London. The seeds of this story were sown when her younger son started making waistcoats for his friends, although fiction quickly took over! Her first adventure, *Skin Deep*, is also available from Lion Publishing.

*To Simon who makes
waistcoats and Violet
who could communicate
without words*

Malcolm
and the Amazing
Technicolor
Waistcoat

Hilary Brand

A LION BOOK

Copyright © 1995 Hilary Brand

The author asserts the moral right
to be identified as the author of this work

Published by
Lion Publishing plc
Sandy Lane West, Oxford, England
ISBN 0 7459 3170 7
Albatross Books Pty Ltd
PO Box 320, Sutherland, NSW 2232, Australia
ISBN 0 7324 0975 6

First edition 1995
First paperback edition 1996
10 9 8 7 6 5 4 3 2 1

A catalogue record for this book is available
from the British Library

Printed and bound in Great Britain
by Cox & Wyman Ltd, Reading

CONTENTS

1

BARGAIN HUNTERS

Going shopping when you've no money is a depressing sort of activity. It's a bit like giving your dreams an airing—you can touch them, try them—but you can't bring them home.

When the Crouch family went shopping, they each had their favourite places to visit. Dad liked the DIY Superstore. He would lovingly handle a power drill or a hot-air paint stripper and lecture Malcolm, if somehow he had managed to drag him along, on the merits of ratchet or non-ratchet screwdrivers.

Mum went to Drabey and Sons, Fine Furniture. She had just decided which three-piece suite to buy when Dad had been made redundant and suddenly the money wasn't there. So now she just came to visit Drabey's, run her hand along the Rose Pink Dralon, and occasionally wonder whether Autumn Brown would be more serviceable, or floral chintz more cheery.

Personally, Malcolm was pleased they'd never got the new suite. He knew what it would have been: 'Take your feet off that, Malcolm,' or 'Eat your chips at the table, Malcolm. I don't want grease on the upholstery.' Malcolm liked the old scruffy sofa with a blanket to hide the torn bits. He couldn't see why it mattered that the other chairs didn't match. He knew it mattered to Mum. But she never said—not now—just went to Drabey's and sighed once in a while.

Malcolm's big sister Stacey had a regular circuit of shops. First was Binns, one of those department stores where the perfume knocks you back when you go in. Stacey liked smelly perfumes. She usually came back with one behind each ear and several more on each wrist. Then the covered market, Sophie's Boutique, and all those fashion chain stores that made Danchester a clone of every other British town.

Stacey had been known to look in Jayne's Bridal-wear, a worrying trend in a sixteen-year-old, even one who had been going out with the same bloke for nearly two years. Then again, the thought of Stacey going off into the sunset as Mrs Matt Bartramm did have its attractions. For a start, her bedroom was bigger than Malcolm's. More importantly she wouldn't be there to tell on him quite so often.

Malcolm had no doubts which were his favourite shops—Mad Mike's Discount Disc Emporium and the Oxfam shop. He'd just been to the first and now he was in the second—and today was a very special day. Today he actually had some money to spend. He'd taken over his friend Razza's free paper round, while Razza went off to Minorca for the summer half term. Malcolm wasn't envious. Who wants to spend a week with their parents without a telly? And anyway, now he had a whole £9.75 to spend.

Or to be accurate, as he sorted through the slightly niffy rails of other people's clothes, he had only £1.37 left. Most had gone on a cassette of Malcolm's very favourite group, Leadbitter Riff, now clutched in a carrier bag; and a little more on a Big Mac, now making its way around his digestive system.

Malcolm had never stopped to think why he liked

second-hand clothes. He just did. He'd never worn the same baggy jeans, lumberjack shirts, trainers or DMs as everyone else. When he was ten, he'd found a tail-coat for 20p in a jumble sale, and embarassed Stacey rotten by wearing it home. He didn't wear it so much now, and he'd gone off his Prince-style frilly shirt— Stacey said he was a big girl's blouse—but he couldn't resist raking through the rails in the hope of finding something wild and wacky.

Nothing much today though. He found an old army coat, and tried it in the mirror. He sighed at the image that stared back. Why couldn't he be tall, dark, myster-ious—not short, sandy-haired and skinny, in a coat six sizes too big?

He was about to give up, when the assistant, a round lady who wore a woolly hat even in summer, came out with an armful of men's clothes and hung them on the rails. *This is more like it,* thought Malcolm. These hadn't belonged to some old grandad. There were jeans with decent labels, silk shirts, baggy jackets and even a Leadbitter Riff T-shirt, but Malcolm had one of those. He looked at the prices and began to wish he hadn't bought the album, or at least the Big Mac. £2 for a shirt, £5 for the best of the jackets, £3.50 for the jeans.

He was about to turn sadly away when he noticed the waistcoat. The back was black silk, but the front was a shimmering mass of colour. It was a rainbow, he realized, arcing across a background of deep blues and purples. Not a child's rainbow of bold brash stripes; this was much more like the real thing. Threads gleamed with gold and silver and blended so subtly that you couldn't quite tell where one colour ended and the next began. Malcolm looked at the price—only £1.25!

Glowing with the thrill of a bargain, he took it to the counter. He even knew when he could wear it. Next Saturday at the school disco. It might be just the thing to make Helena notice him at last. Helena Pinchin had moved to Danchester and joined Year 9 last term. Malcolm was only in her set for biology, where he sat behind her and gazed adoringly at her red-dyed hair. He thought about soppy things like kissing, that only a year ago he swore he'd never do. Malcolm was thirteen and girls were overtaking football as the meaning of life. He found himself looking at them a lot and thinking exciting but disturbing thoughts about the shapes beneath their school uniforms. Not Helena, of course. She was a goddess and his love for her was pure and undefiled. Well, almost.

Malcolm went out deeply satisfied—an excellent bargain, a great album, a digested Big Mac and 12p in change. As he left, two men went in. He didn't notice them. What he was seeing was himself and Helena out on the bench at the back of the CDT block, together in the balmy moonlight.

But the men were quite noticeable. One was big with yellowy straw-like hair, a square jaw and a big scar on one cheek. The other was black, dressed in a black satin bomber jacket, and with a face permanently scowling, like a boxer psyching himself up for a match. They seemed to know what they were looking for. They headed straight for the men's rails and pounced on the stash of clothes Vera Smalley had just brought in. *Know a bargain when they see one*, thought Vera. She sighed. She would have loved to have seen her Albert in one of those shirts, but all his life he'd stuck to his white drip-dry. The two men scooped up armfuls of clothes and went to the counter.

'This was all one load, right?'

'Er, yes,' said Vera uncertainly. They were leaning forward as if to accuse her, and Scowler was making her nervous.

'Just come in, right?'

'Er, yes, a few hours ago. We've had to price them. Nice, aren't they?' she ventured. 'You got here just in time. We're the best charity shop in town, you know. All the quality stuff comes to us.'

Working in Oxfam on Tuesdays, Thursdays and Fridays was the high spot of Vera's lonely week, and she did it with pride.

'Anything else, or is this it?' demanded Scarface.

'Oh er, yes, er, no. There was one thing, a waistcoat. A young lad just bought it.'

Scarface gripped the counter. 'Who was he? Where'd he go?'

'Um, I, er, I'm not . . . I didn't see.'

Scowler had his hands in his pockets. Vera remembered films of men who pointed their pockets at innocent retailers. There could be a gun in there.

She had a sudden burst of inspiration. 'He was wearing a school blazer. Now I think about it, I did recognize the badge. It was Sedgehill. No, not that one. Danchester Boys, now was it? I'm sure I ought to remember. I used to be a schools' nurse, you see, before I retired.' Vera looked up hopefully. She was always pleased to reminisce to anyone who would listen. Something about the two men's faces told her that now was not the time. 'Ah yes, it's coming to me . . . Wait . . . Yes, Broad Heath Comprehensive, that's it. I'm sure of it.' She beamed with delight. Her memory was nothing like as bad as her daughter-in-law claimed. 'Broad Heath. Definitely.'

'So where's that then?' asked Scowler.

'Well, Broad Heath, of course,' said Vera puzzled. It dawned on her that the men might not be local. 'It's an

11

estate, nice little houses, no high-rise, about a mile out of town on the Pogshaw Road. You could get the 57 bus from the depot, but I don't know if . . .'

The two men had already taken their armfuls of clothes and were racing from the shop.

Vera's knees trembled. She felt as if she'd just survived a heist. She had, she realized. They hadn't paid.

Vera decided she must be brave and forceful. 'Stop thief!' she bleated as their backs disappeared around the corner into Danbury Plaza.

Dad was in his armchair when Malcolm got back. That wasn't unusual. It was where he always was these days. And he was doing what he always did at 5.30, watching 'Buzzword'. Dad liked quiz games.

Before—when watching was a way of winding down after a hard day's work—he would bellow out the answers, thumping the arm of the chair like a buzzer, and telling nearly every contestant that he or she was a 'lame-brained twit'.

Today he just sat there, slumped and blank-eyed. He grunted as Malcolm went through the living-room. Most of their conversations were grunts these days, unless Dad discovered something Malcolm had done that he didn't like. Grunts were safer.

Malcolm tiptoed past and up to his room to try his new album. He slotted in the cassette and put his cowboy-booted feet up on to the bed. He turned the amp up as near to full volume as he dared. He closed his eyes and thought about Helena for a moment or two. His mind went to Danchester's away game at Ipswich last week (not a happy thought) and from there, via a wandering chain of ideas, to Leadbitter Riff's last concert at Wembley. The very last. There would never be another.

Malcolm sighed and opened his eyes. He fished in the

carrier for the free music paper the record shop gave out. He thumbed past the ads and the new releases to the article he wanted: 'Tragic story of Riff's last stand'.

It carried the story of Riff Pritchett's death from an overdose, old news now, but still shocking to Malcolm as he read it. It also had some new news. Drongo Leadbitter's announcement that he was leaving the business.

> '*The rock scene's turned sour on me,*' claimed Drongo, adding that it was time for him to find a new lifestyle. Quite what this lifestyle would be, he was not saying, only that it would be a million miles from sex, drugs and rock 'n' roll. What may be a good move for rock dinosaur Drongo, looking distinctly raddled and shaky after the coroner's verdict on his friend's death, will be bad news for rock fans.
>
> '*There can be no more Leadbitter Riff,*' said Drongo. '*Any attempt to carry on would be a sort of heresy.*' Even the last album, completed just before Pritchett's death, has been scrapped, although Leadbitter in a mysterious statement asserted that under certain circumstances it may yet see the light of day. '*It's buried,*' said Drongo. '*Silent music. Hidden deep. Only someone with a simple lifestyle and an eye for beauty will ever discover its whereabouts. If they can find it, it's theirs.*' Drongo says that the album and all its sales profits will be the property of the lucky finder, but is giving no clues as to its whereabouts. Drongo himself is now missing, but is rumoured to be on a Caribbean island . . .

Malcolm sighed again. Even Danchester's prospects for the Cup were less depressing than this. No more Leadbitter Riff. He turned the volume up in angry protest.

Downstairs the front door banged. 6.13. Mum in from the supermarket. 'Malco-o-o-lm, turn that thing down.'

Footsteps on the landing, Mum going to change her overall. A knock on Malcolm's door, 6.22, right on cue. 'I hope you're doing your homework,' Malcolm mouthed it along with her.

'Yes, Mum,' he said out loud, rummaging in his school bag for his diary.

6.58. 'Supper,' called Mum. Dad liked food on the table at half past six, but these days he was very patient. He just sat there and waited while Mum heated up the quickest thing she could think of after a day on the checkout. He didn't complain now, and Stacey had stopped quoting from her 'Women in Society' history project. Mealtimes were an uneasy truce.

Malcolm decided to wear his waistcoat to supper. *Liven the place up*. That was a mistake.

'Whad'you call that?' asked Dad, barely glancing up from his sausages.

'It's called a waistcoat,' said Stacey helpfully, pumping diet ketchup over her beans. 'Honestly, Malc, you look a right poser.'

'Bit of a nancy, I'd call it,' grumped Dad. 'When are you going to stop wearing those cissy-boy clothes? Waste of good money.'

'It only cost £1.25.'

'Junk shop again, I suppose. It's bad enough being unemployed, without having a son who goes round in other people's cast-offs. Have a bit of self-respect.'

'There's no shame, Bob,' said Mum, forking her sausage, always a smaller portion than everyone else. 'Even quite posh folks buy at charity shops now. Anyway, I think it's nice.'

There is nothing more calculated to make you turn against your clothes than if your mum thinks they're 'nice'. Malcolm gritted his teeth.

'Very pretty embroidery,' continued Mum.

'For a woman,' growled Dad.

Malcolm changed the subject. 'Can we watch "Top of the Pops"?'

'No,' said Dad, in a voice like a jail door shutting. 'You know your mum likes "Emmerdale".'

So do you, thought Malcolm. *You're turning into a soap junkie, but you'd never admit it.*

That just about sums up my life, he decided, making a mushy mountain of potato, beans and brown sauce. *Always 'Emmerdale' and never 'Top of the Pops'.*

After supper, Stacey went round to Matt's and Malcolm escaped to his room. He put on his headphones and turned the amp up full blast. He did ten minutes of maths and four sentences of English, then stopped. *The greatest musicians of our generation gone for ever,* he mused, fishing for a felt pen, and writing 'Leadbitter Riff for ever' on his school bag. He'd promised Mum he wouldn't graffiti this bag, but whoever heard of a school bag without graffiti?

He was so absorbed in the lettering and the music that he didn't hear the row. He did feel the door slam, but it was only when he came downstairs, for a cup of tea and a pocketful of biscuits, that he noticed Mum's red eyes and Dad's empty chair.

'Where's Dad?'

'Your father's gone down the pub.'

'Oh, well, that's good.' Mum was always saying Dad ought to get out more.

'No, it's not,' said Mum curtly. 'He's drinking my new shoes.'

Malcolm's brow furrowed, then relaxed into a smile. 'That was quite witty for you, Mum.'

Mum quivered for a moment, then lowered her head into her hands. Her shoulders heaved and she allowed herself one deep breath that ended in a sob.

15

'Sorry, Mum, I didn't mean . . .'

But the dam had burst, and Mum sobbed wildly, on and on. Malcolm had never seen her do that before, not even when Grandma died.

He didn't know what you were supposed to do at times like this. He thought you made cups of tea, so he put the kettle on.

'It's not your fault,' said Mum eventually with a big shuddering sigh. Suddenly she rushed out the back, but it was only to return with a length of loo roll for her eyes.

'It's your dad, the pig-headed pig.'

Malcolm was about to say that pigs could hardly be anything other than pig-headed, but thought better of it.

'Still, it's not really his fault either. All those years at the engineering works and then . . . nothing. But he's his own worst enemy . . . I was only trying to help. It seemed like a good idea. And now what am I going to do?'

She blew her nose loudly. 'The trouble is, I promised.'

'Promised what, Mum?'

'Oh, I don't know. It's hopeless.' Mum buried her head and cried some more. Malcolm made a cup of tea. He brought it to the table and awkwardly patted her still-heaving shoulders.

'Promised what, Mum?'

She looked up as if surprised to see him there. 'Oh Malcolm, take no notice. I'm just tired.'

'Yes, but promised what?'

'Oh, it's just that your dad's so bored, I thought it would do him good to get out. So I went to the Volunteer Agency—you know, they put people in touch with other people who need help. And anyway, they told me about this old lady who lives just round the corner and how her garden needs doing. I said Dad would go.

And they phoned her up then and there, and she was so delighted that someone would be coming. And then I told Dad and . . .' She burst into tears again.

Malcolm could imagine. Ever since Dad had been made redundant eighteen months ago, he'd got steadily more depressed. He started off bright and determined. 'Positive mental attitude,' he said. 'It's good,' he said —now he'd have time to catch up on all the things he'd missed. But he never caught up. For a while he'd tried. He stripped the walls in the living-room, but then they couldn't afford the wallpaper. He read books with titles like *How to Sell Yourself* or *New Life in Mid-Life*. He scoured the job ads and wrote millions of letters. 'With your skills, you'll be working in no time,' said Mum. But Dad knew better. 'Everyone uses computers now,' he said, and it seemed he was right.

So now he just sat, grumpy and glued to the box. Dad was making an art form out of being grumpy. Anyone making helpful suggestions as to what he could do— well, that was like throwing a match in a fireworks factory. Whoosh!

And Mum had just thrown one.

'Look, Mum.' Malcolm heard something strangely like his own voice. 'Don't worry about this old lady.'

Malcolm! Malc baby, said his inner voice, *I can't believe you're saying this*. Malcolm ignored it. He could feel himself forming the words, one of the biggest whoppers ever to have passed his lips: 'I don't mind gardening.' *There, done now, lumbered*. 'I'll go on Saturday, before the match.'

2

BATTY PRUNE

Malcolm woke and remembered it was Saturday. Saturday was a Big Day. Football this morning—and tonight the disco. It wasn't just that Malcolm enjoyed kicking a ball and dancing—he wasn't sure he did enjoy dancing—but these were Important Events. Events that could shape his destiny.

It wasn't exactly a big match—a friendly between Broad Heath and Landau Boys—but rumour had it that the scout for Danchester United Juniors was going to be there.

Malcolm's Grandad had once tried out for Danchester United, but then the war came. 'Bloomin' 'Itler ruined me chances, but you, lad, you've got the touch. I can tell. You'll be the legend in this family.'

And hadn't the *Mercury* once mentioned Malcolm's 'useful' defence in the Stanley Figgins Junior Schools' Memorial Cup?

And then the disco—another date with destiny. Helena, dark and mysterious, with eyes for him alone.

Malcolm leapt up early. Over two bowls of Weetabix and four slices of bread and jam, he thought about what to wear tonight.

Black jeans, he decided, black shirt and the waistcoat. He went up to his bedroom to try. He surveyed himself in the mirror. Not bad. He put on a cassette, tried gelling his hair back, and moved rhythmically to the music. Had to get it right—seductive with just a hint of menace. Yes, very cool. Oh, that zit on his chin—but then the lights would be low. They *would* be low, wouldn't they?

The waistcoat was a bit crumpled, he noticed. Perhaps he'd give it an iron. He transferred the cassette to his Walkman and went downstairs to put up the ironing board. He thrust his hips in time to the pulsating music. No one else was up. He swayed as he ironed.

'Love this bit.' He took off in a rave, iron in hand. He got tangled in the lead and put it down, dancing wildly, arms punching the air. He became a rock guitarist, bouncing sideways across an imaginary stage and finishing the last insistent chord with a huge flourish.

The music stopped and he noticed the smell. He went back and picked up the iron. A huge hole, the iron's neat imprint, lay smack in the middle of the waistcoat's silky back.

'Bloomin', bloomin', bloomin', bloomin'... Rude Words!' muttered Malcolm and kicked the ironing board. The iron toppled. Malcolm caught it, but the hotplate burned his knuckles.

Positive mental attitude, he told himself as he numbed his fingers under the cold tap. *Stupid waistcoat. Wasn't that special. Only cost £1.25.* He wasn't fooling himself. It wasn't only £1.25, it was a dream. It was Malcolm the strutting disco king, the one the girls whispered and giggled about. He had shrivelled away like the silk on the waistcoat into Malcolm the zitty thirteen-year-old who never had new clothes and didn't have the nerve to dance. The whispers and giggles turned to sneers and sniggers.

Malcolm unplugged the iron. He went to throw the waistcoat in the bin, then changed his mind. He chucked it on his bedroom floor and picked up his football kit.

Mum was in the kitchen when he came down.

'Goin' to Marty's to watch videos,' mumbled Malcolm. 'After the match, we're going to Razza's. I'll go to the disco from there. Don't bother about food.'

There is a technique to these things. You wait until you're just ready to go out and Mum and Dad are busy. On the phone or paying the milkman are ideal. Then you tell them you won't be back all day, and with luck you're out of the door before they remember to tell you to tidy your room or do your history essay or visit Grandad or go shopping for school trousers.

Today Malcolm was out of luck. 'Oh, but . . .' Mum lowered her voice. 'What about Mrs Walenski?'

'Who?'

Mum looked round anxiously but Dad was still snoring upstairs. 'The old lady—with the garden. You did say you'd go.'

Malcolm groaned. 'But Mu-u-u-um!' His voice rose like the whine of a jet engine.

Mum ran an anxious, soapy hand through her hair. 'She's expecting someone. I put a note through her door saying Saturday.'

Malcolm noticed how grey the shadows were under her eyes. He brought his cereal bowl to the sink and looked hopefully out of the window. 'It might rain.' The sky was disgustingly clear.

Malcolm stomped out of the kitchen.

'Malcolm?' queried his mother. Her voice had that pitiful edge he hated.

'Oh, all right.' He dumped his football kit and went snarling out of the front door.

Gloomily he made his way to Mrs Walenski's. It was just around the corner, a tiny bungalow that Malcolm had never noticed before. He saw now that honeysuckle almost obliterated the front door. Rose bushes sprawled fierce and rampant through the front garden. A blue-flowering plant crept and spread like a mat beneath.

What's she want a gardener for? Personally, Malcolm liked gardens like that. Much better than neat ones like their neighbours', the Sedges, with one marigold planted exactly every 15 centimetres along the path. He'd even seen Percy Sedge take out a ruler to get it right.

On Mrs Walenski's front door was a faded note in spidery writing. 'Please come round side. Knock and wait.'

He ducked his way under a rickety trellis to the side door. He knocked. Nothing. No sound but the distant bypass and a wasp buzzing round the dustbins. Good, she must be out. He knocked again, a token knock. Mentally he was already round at Marty's with his feet up in front of 'Death Ride to Thunder City'.

Then he heard it. Deep inside the bungalow a strange shuffling noise. Shuffle, clunk, shuffle, clunk. He began to see movement through the cobbled glass—a bent figure creeping nearer.

Eventually the door opened and he looked down into Mrs Walenski's face. It was a shrivelled prune of a face, framed in wispy white hair. She looked at him suspiciously. There were a few wispy whiskers on her chin.

'Gardening—I've come to do the gardening.'

She waved a misshapen hand towards him. 'You come,' she said. 'Garden, time chop back... boy... Come in.'

Can't even talk proper, thought Malcolm as he followed her slowly shuffle-clunking her walking frame up the dingy corridor. *S'pose she's foreign.*

He followed her into the sitting room, adjusting his eyes to the gloom. Only a few strands of sunlight pushed their way through the purple-flowered creeper that covered the French windows. They had obviously not been opened for a long time.

Inside there were plants too. Plants on high shelves that trailed down to the floor. Plants on the floor that meandered up to the ceiling. Drapes hung everywhere. A filmy fabric dotted with sequins covered the lamp shade. The patterned velvet curtains were looped back with huge, gold-tasselled cords. A shawl with long silver fringes was thrown across a sofa.

Spooky, thought Malcolm. *Perhaps she's a fortune teller—or a witch!*

Where there weren't drapes there were photos—some brown and faded, some black and white, some with scrawling signatures across the corner. The people who smiled from them clearly thought they were something. Women in beaded frocks with feathers in their hair. Men with white scarves and top hats at a jaunty angle. Women with flowing skirts, tiny waists and absurd little saucer hats. Portraits of people by now long gone, or else as faded and shrivelled as their owner.

'You like?'

'Er, yes.' Malcolm realized he was staring.

'My cly... My cly... I dress... clothes...'

Great, thought Malcolm. *She's not just foreign, she's batty as well. Let's just do the gardening and get out of here.*

'About your garden, Mrs Walenski,' he said loudly and slowly in the sort of voice people reserve for foreigners, idiots or the deaf. Mrs Walenski appeared to be all three.

She wasn't listening to him now, but leafing through a big red desk diary. She passed it to him, open at the front.

'I have had a stroke,' it said in spidery scrawl. 'I cannot speak very well. I also have arthritis.'

Glad we've got that sorted, thought Malcolm, *whatever a stroke is.*

Mrs Walenski was pointing to her knees. 'Arthritis,' she said. 'Pla . . . Pla . . .'

Oh no, here we go again, thought Malcolm.

'Plastic,' said Mrs Walenski triumphantly.

Right, she's got a stroke and plastic knees. That's it, she really is batty.

'Look, Mrs Walenski, about this gardening . . .'

It could have been worse. She took him outside and showed him a battered electric lawnmower in a dank coal house. Mowing was OK. You didn't have to worry about which were weeds and which were flowers. Malcolm turned on his Walkman and mindlessly pushed the mower up and down. The grass, almost knee high in places, came down in a satisfying sweep. Only the thistles stubbornly lay down under the mower, popping up defiantly behind. 'Think you can fool me?' muttered Malcolm, mowing nonchalantly in the other direction, then turning to take a sudden run at them. Only a few withstood surprise attack and these he pulled up at the roots, with a 'Hah. Gotcha.'

It didn't take long. Mrs Walenski's garden was hardly a football pitch—a goal mouth or two at the most. Malcolm surveyed his work. Not quite a velvet, smooth turf, more a patchy stubble—but no longer a jungle.

Malcolm put the mower away with Leadbitter Riff still pounding in his ears. He shut the coal house door, then jumped. Mrs Walenski and her frame were right behind him. 'Cuppa tea.'

'Thanks but really I must get . . .'

Oh no! It really wasn't a question. The tea was already in the pot, knitted teacosy on top. There was milk in a jug and sugar lumps with tongs. She peered hopefully

23

at him with sad watery eyes. Malcolm noticed a plateful of Jaffa cakes behind her. *Oh well . . .* and he had to admit he was thirsty. *OK, it's worth another batty conversation.*

Malcolm carried the tray to Mrs Walenski's table. Her upright armchair sat beside it, a large dining table covered with everything she could possibly need— books, cassettes, orange squash, bottles of pills, a biscuit barrel, a bowl of fruit, a phone and the TV remote control. For those things furthest away she used a long stick with pincers at the end.

She used them now to push the Jaffa cakes towards him. 'You eat,' she said.

Malcolm ate and gulped the hot tea in an effort to be gone. He peered at the nearest photo, a lady in a jewelled gown. It was signed, Malcolm noticed, 'To darling Eva'.

'My fa . . .' said Mrs Walenski.

Oh no, not again.

'My fa . . . fa . . . fa . . .'

'Family?' tried Malcolm helpfully.

Mrs Walenski shook her head emphatically. 'Fa . . . Fa . . .'

'Father?' tried Malcolm.

'No, no,' said Mrs Walenski helplessly. 'Fa . . .'

'Famous!' said Malcolm. 'They're famous people.'

'Ah ye-e-s,' said Mrs Walenski doubtfully, then, 'No-o-o, my fa . . . fa . . .'

She picked up her pincers and drew towards her a dog-eared photo album. 'Fa . . .' she said triumphantly and thrust it towards him. The first page had black and white photos cut out of a magazine. The caption read:

Society dressmaker Eva Walenski showed her first collection this month after leaving Hartnell's illustrious salon. Her exquisite use of fabrics and attention to detail

24

meant the clothes were snapped up quickly by the
fashionable set of Kensington and Chelsea.

'Fashion!' said Malcolm.

'Ah, fashion!' repeated Mrs Walenski, a broad beam spreading over her wrinkled features.

Malcolm turned the page. A photo showed a tiny lady with swept-back, black hair, pinning the sleeve of a tall, willowy model. 'Is that you,' asked Malcolm, 'the little one?'

'Me,' agreed Mrs Walenski.

'You used to make clothes?'

'Make clothes,' repeated Mrs Walenski. 'Look.'

Malcolm looked. The album was filled with glossy photos of models. Long satin ballgowns encrusted with jewels. A bridal gown frilled with lace. A slim, tailored suit in black and white, curling feathers embroidered down the front.

'Very nice,' said Malcolm, flipping the pages and thinking how sad it was that someone from this glamorous world had shrunk to a batty old prune in Broad Heath.

He turned over to where a woman in black floaty chiffon held the arm of a man in a bow tie and satin waistcoat. That reminded him.

'I've got a waistcoat,' he said, to fill the silence, 'but I've just ruined it.'

Mrs Walenski looked up enquiringly.

'Put the iron through the back of it. Made a dirty great hole.'

Mrs Walenski chuckled. 'Dirty great hole,' she repeated.

'Ruined it,' said Malcolm, wistfully.

'No, no, you mend,' said Mrs Walenski.

'Nah, not me. Wouldn't know how.'

'I help,' insisted Mrs Walenski. She picked up her pincer stick and pointed it towards a cupboard.

'You look,' she said.

Malcolm went to the cupboard. *Now what?* He wished he'd never mentioned anything. Inside the cupboard was a sewing machine, quite a new one, and lots of cardboard boxes. Mrs Walenski pointed her stick at one on a bottom shelf. In it were stuffed heaps of fabric. Silks and satins in all manner of colours.

'You mend,' said Mrs Walenski. 'I show how.'

'Oh no, really, it's all right.' Malcolm picked up the last Jaffa cake and stood up to go.

'You bring,' she insisted. 'We do.'

'Not now?'

'Yes. Now, you bring. We mend.'

'Well, not really, I've got a football match, you see. Anyway, I was going to wear it tonight. I'd never get it done now, so it doesn't much matter.'

'Tonight,' said Mrs Walenski, glancing at the big clock framed with cherubs that stood on the mantelpiece. 'Yes, tonight. One hour, two. I show—you do.'

'No, really, it doesn't matter.'

'Pah,' Mrs Walenski thumped the table.

'Look, I've got to go now. Football. I'll try and bring it later, OK? I'll come round after the match.'

Phew. Malcolm blinked at the sunlight. *I'm not going back in there*. He headed for Broadmeadow Fields, and his chance of glory.

'It wasn't fair. I could have done it. Could have stopped him. He was bigger than me. He played dirty. He's a dirty, snobby, smarmy git.'

They were a snobby lot, the Landau Boys, and none snobbier than their new attacker. Casually he strolled on to the pitch, casually he flicked back his blond hair and cracked his knuckles. Casually he kneed Malcolm into blinding agony, and casually he scored a goal.

'Foul,' cried Malcolm. 'Dirty rat.' But no one else had seen.

'Gotta admit that's some nifty footwork,' said Si Parker, at half time. 'The guy's a natural.'

Huh, thought Malcolm. *So'm I.*

The second half got better. He gave Mr Snobby Landau a satisfying kick behind the knees, and managed to put himself between the ball and the net enough to get a few cheers.

Just luck, though, he told himself honestly. 'Just luck,' he told the others modestly.

'That bloke, the one with the cap. I saw him looking at you. He wrote something down,' said Marty.

'Yeah, "Awful hair gel",' said Si.

But Malcolm glowed.

Already he saw his name on Danchester United's Junior try-out list. He saw himself in the reserves, the first team, making that final save at Wembley, hoisted on his team-mates' shoulders, sponsoring trainers . . .

'I am a champion,' he sang to himself and went off to play Nintendo with Razza.

But Razza was out. 'Gone to see someone,' said his mum. 'Malcolm, I think.'

Malcolm headed home. No one in, no sign of Razza. Malcolm switched on the telly, burnt some toast, and tipped his muddy kit on the floor alongside the waistcoat. He turned the waistcoat over sadly in his hands. He thought about the batty prune. He couldn't help seeing those sad hopeful eyes. He picked up the waistcoat and went out.

'Once she sees it, she'll know it's hopeless,' thought Malcolm as he knocked on the honeysuckle-covered door.

Mrs Walenski looked at the waistcoat. 'Easy done,' she chuckled and ushered him in. She rifled through her boxes of fabrics and came up with a black silk dotted with tiny diamonds. 'OK?' she asked.

'Yes, OK,' said Malcolm, 'but . . .'

'You lift.' She pointed to the sewing machine.

'Now thread.' She gestured to a tin marked Peek Frean's Biscuits. It was full of cotton reels.

She expects me to thread a sewing machine? thought Malcolm.

She did, but pointing to each bit in turn made it far easier than he'd expected. Then she handed him a tiny forked metal prong. 'Unpick,' she said.

Malcolm thought about how frustrated she must feel as he clumsily unpicked the waistcoat's seams. He looked at her hands, lumpen and twisted, and tried to imagine them smooth and straight, whizzing fabric through the machine. He glanced at her cloudy eyes and wondered when they last saw well enough to push a needle into an intricate design. He wondered what it was like, the day she finally decided it was over. She met his gaze.

'Come, come, don't stop,' she chided. 'We finish today.'

And they did. Malcolm became Mrs Walenski's hands, and she became his brain as they cut, pinned, tacked and machined together. 'You good,' she told him as he cut out. 'Very good,' she said as he sewed. 'This boy, a natural,' she proclaimed as he pressed seams.

There was only one point when Malcolm began to think Mrs Walenski really was batty after all. She had made him turn the waistcoat inside out and stitch until it seemed impossible that it could ever turn the right way out again. *Very useful,* thought Malcolm. *She's mended it, but it's permanently inside out.*

And then suddenly, the sewing was finished. All except one tiny gap. 'Push through,' she insisted, and he did, miraculously pulling all the waistcoat right way out through the tiny gap. It looked as good as new.

'That's brilliant,' said Malcolm.

'Ah,' said Mrs Walenski and sat back beaming with pride. 'You like needlework?' she asked hopefully.

'Yes,' said Malcolm, to his surprise. ''s'not bad.'

Just a little hand-sewing and it was all done. Malcolm was knotting the last stitch on the waistcoat when something fluttered out from its pocket. It was a piece of paper. He picked it up from the floor and read:

> *Down beneath Old Harry's Seat*
> *Down behind Old Harry's feet*
> *Silent music where waters flow*
> *Hidden where strangers never go*

Well, it must have meant something to somebody, thought Malcolm, putting it aside on the table. *I wonder who had this waistcoat before me?*

He put it on and admired himself in Mrs Walenski's gold-curlicued mirror.

'You come,' said Mrs Walenski. 'You come again. I make you great couturier.'

A great what? thought Malcolm. 'Dunno about that, but OK, I'll come again.'

Mrs Walenski's beam lit up her face. 'Really?'

'Yeah, honest. I promise.'

'Name? Phone?'

Malcolm wrote his name and address on the scrap of paper she handed him. She added it to a pile of similar scraps on her table.

The cherub clock chimed. 7.30. Twenty minutes to go home and shower, and ten minutes to school. Just in time for the disco—amazing. Malcolm smiled to himself in the mirror. He was going to the disco and he was looking good.

3

DISCO KING

Malcolm's first mistake was going home to change his shirt. Cousin Jeffrey was in the kitchen. Cousin Jeffrey was nineteen going on thirty-five. He wore purple and blue shell suits with black shoes and white socks. Jeffrey worked for the Post Office and went to church three times a week. He thought Cliff Richard was the greatest rock musician of all time and that Terry Venables presented a 'yoof' programme on Channel 4. He and Malcolm did not get on too well.

Malcolm tried tiptoeing up the stairs, but Mum had heard the door. 'Malcolm, is that you? Jeffrey's here.'

Malcolm shuffled unwillingly into the kitchen. 'Jeffrey's come to invite you to ... What is it, Jeffrey, some kind of event?'

'Yes, er, yes, Malcolm, it's our first PIG event tonight. It's especially aimed at "unchurched" youth, so I felt sure you'd be just the person to invite.' He noticed Malcolm's lowered jaw. 'Oh yes, silly me,' he chuckled. 'PIG stands for Partners In Gospel. Of course it would have been better to be Partners In The Gospel, but PITG doesn't trip off the tongue quite the same, does it? So ...' He noticed Malcolm's jaw was still dropped, and slowed to a halt.

'Great, Jeffrey, I'd love to,' put in Malcolm quickly, 'but I'm going to the school disco.'

'School disco!' said Mum, tipping off the ginger nuts she'd just put on a plate. 'You didn't tell me. You know I don't like those things.'

That's why I didn't tell you, thought Malcolm.

'I did tell you—this morning,' he said.

'There was a knife fight last year.'

'Mum, it was two girls with a school dinner knife. You can't even cut burgers with them.'

'And drugs—they have drugs at these things.'

'Oh Mum, that's just a rumour.' It was probably true, but that wasn't the point. There were drugs at school any day of the week if you knew where to look. 'And there's no booze, just a soft drinks bar.'

'I still think you'd be better going with Jeffrey. He's come all this way to get you.'

I don't want to be 'got', thought Malcolm. He'd been to one of these do's before. At the end they played soft music and told everyone who was a sinner to come up the front.

'I'd make sure he'd be back by 10.30, Auntie,' said Jeffrey.

Creep, thought Malcolm.

'And that's another thing,' said Mum, 'these school do's go on till all hours.'

'Come on, Mum, I've promised my friends I'd go. I won't be late, honest. Look, I'll be in by 11 o'clock, promise.' What was he saying?!

Mum sighed in resignation. 'Well, I suppose I can't force you . . .'

Malcolm sighed with relief.

' . . . though I'm sure Jeffrey's event would have been far more suitable. Just don't get into trouble, that's all.'

Jeffrey sighed at the failure to secure his 'un-churched' youth, but there was one thing you could say about Jeffrey—he never gave up. 'Oh well, there's another one next month. We're having a spaghetti-eating contest. You'll like that.'

'Great,' said Malcolm. He made a mental note to be out of the country that day.

Phew, made it, thought Malcolm, as he stood on the corner waiting for his mates. He ran through his entrance to the disco. He would pause at the top of the steps that led down into the school hall. The girls would look up and smile secret smiles, each feeling that he was the one for her. But there was only one for him—Helena. Across the hall their eyes would meet. As he descended, she would rise and move gracefully in slow motion towards him . . .

'Wanna chip?' asked Razza loudly behind his left ear.

'You're late,' said Malcolm.

'Went down the chippy,' said Jamie Bond unnecessarily.

'And the offy,' said Si Parker with a smirk.

'Like yer waistcoat,' said Marty Braithwaite.

'Yeah,' agreed the others. 'Neat.'

On the way up the hill they discussed their intended conquests.

'I bet I get off with Mandy Trumpet,' said Jamie.

'That's not difficult.' said Si. 'Last year she snogged with twenty blokes in one evening. It's a well-known fact. And she only knew ten of them.'

'Bet you can't,' said Razza.

'OK, 50p says I can.'

'I'm going for Sonya Harding, myself,' said Marty. 'Her friend says she likes me.'

Malcolm kept his preference to himself. He had his reasons to hope. After all, hadn't she turned round in biology last week and said, 'You goin' to the disco, Malc?' He had treasured those words, rolling them round his mind, hearing again every lilting cadence in his dreams.

And now he was here. At the top of the steps they paused. Lights flashed and music thumped. A few lack-lustre figures danced in the middle of the vast space. Many more hung around the walls. No one looked at Malcolm and his friends, except Mr Robinson who was on bouncer duty by the door. 'No drink, no drugs, no knives,' he recited. 'Show me your pockets, boys.'

They complied.

'All right. Crouch, let's see your socks.'

'Sir?'

'Your socks, boy. Roll your trousers up.'

Malcolm had never been to the disco before. Was this some strange kind of initiation ceremony? Mr Robinson was not the sort of teacher you argued with. Malcolm rolled up his trousers.

'Aha, cowboy boots. Get 'em off, lad.'

Now people were starting to look. Malcolm went hot and cold with embarassment. 'But sir.'

'Come on, lad. Spot checks. Have to do them.'

'No sir, they're not spots, they're...' Malcolm remembered exactly which socks he had on. All the rest, the sophisticated plain black ones, were in the washing machine. Mum had scooped up the dirty heap under his bed this morning. In the absence of any others, Malcolm was wearing the bright green musical Father Christmas socks that Auntie Grace had given him last year.

People were looking now. Frantically Malcolm scoured the hall, hoping that Helena was turned the other way. He saw her. She looked up and smiled. She even gave a little wave. And then she giggled. He definitely saw her giggle. Suddenly the music stopped. Robbie, the sixth former on the disco, was desperately turning knobs. Mr Robinson bent down to check Malcolm's socks.

Everything else stopped in a huge silence—and in the midst of it, suddenly a tinny little tune began to play. 'Jingle bells, Jingle bells . . .' It was Malcolm's musical socks.

After about half an hour, Malcolm's face had stopped burning and he plucked up courage to look out from the corner where he had hidden. Everyone else thought it was a great joke, of course. Even Helena. He'd seen her choking with laughter, and wished he could die.

The others knew exactly what Mr Robinson was up to. 'Booze. People smuggle it in. Old Robbo's got eyes like a hawk. The only way to get it past him is to stuff a bottle down your sock.'

'Like this,' said Si Parker. Surreptitiously he pushed up his jeans and pulled out two miniature bottles labelled Navy Rum.

'Or this,' said Marty, and took one Beefeater Gin from each leg. 'My Dad gets them free from customers,' he explained mysteriously.

'Go on, you need some,' said Si, uncapping the bottle and passing it to Malcolm.

Well, what would you do after such a humiliation? Malcolm took a swig. He choked, coughed and spluttered and a warm glow spread down his throat and around his body. He took another swig. It tasted like medicine, but it worked a lot quicker. Si opened the second bottle. Malcolm took another gulp, and then several more.

Jamie was already hanging around Mandy Trumpet, and now Marty went off to try his luck with Sonya Harding. Si tagged along. Razza—solid, bespectacled Razza—didn't like girls. He liked chess and football

34

and Dungeons and Dragons. Malcolm was glad of his company.

He looked around. Helena wasn't far away, just sitting watching the DJ. One or two boys had come up to her, but she hadn't seemed interested. All the usual crowd were here—Year 9 upwards. Over beyond Helena, Malcolm noticed a couple of fellows he hadn't seen before. They looked too old even for sixth formers. One had yellow straw-like hair and a scar down one cheek. The other, a black guy, wore a shiny black bomber jacket. He stared around the hall, scowling at everyone. Something caught his eye in Malcolm's direction. Was it Malcolm, or Helena in between? *He's eyeing up Helena, I'm sure he is,* thought Malcolm. Scowler bent and said something to his colleague. Scarface glanced up and nodded.

That's it. I'm not having thugs like that after her, thought Malcolm. He stood up. For a moment the world spun alarmingly. 'Oi, Ražza, gimme a drink.' Razza had become guardian of the bottles.

Malcolm took another swig, gin this time. More like perfume than medicine, but it had the same effect. Malcolm stood up again, slowly this time and clinging on to the chair. He was alarmed to see the two thugs stand up too. Helena also stood up, completely unaware and made her way on to the floor in the direction of the DJ. The swaying mass of people swallowed her up. The men hesitated. Malcolm plunged into the crowd in the direction Helena had gone, crashing into people as he went.

It seemed amazingly hard to go in a straight line. People pushed him back. Mandy Trumpet caught hold of him and danced up close. Malcolm pulled himself away. The two men were up, following Malcolm, trying to look as if they were casually dancing in his direction. Malcolm danced too, drifting nonchalantly towards Helena. Helena, however, moved on, joining another group of friends and working her way further towards the disc jockey. Malcolm headed towards her. The two men followed. They drifted their way around the hall like a swirl on a weather map, until Helena reached the disco unit. Casually she leaned against it and smiled at the DJ. Rave Robbie smiled back.

He could be her brother, hoped Malcolm.

Helena leaned on the disco unit and stared dreamily at the dancers.

Go for broke, thought Malcolm and danced up in front of her. Funny, he'd always felt shy about dancing before, but now a sort of what-the-heck feeling was coming over him. He threw himself around in his Michael Jackson lookalike style. Helena laughed and clapped him on.

I always knew I was a good dancer at heart, thought Malcolm, spinning on one heel. Others around him clapped and cheered. He was getting dizzy, but stopping seemed incredibly hard. No problem, he could go on for ever.

He didn't. The music stopped abruptly again. (This was the fourth time and Robbie had discovered the reason. Couples going into a dark corner kept tripping over the lead and pulling the mains plug out.) Robbie got up and yelled into the corner.

Malcolm, spinning wildly, tried to stop, failed and fell headlong. Someone caught him. His head was cradled in a soft scented bosom. He looked up and his eyes met Helena's deep green ones. It was an electric moment.

'You're a nut, Malcolm Crouch,' she said, with, he thought, a touch of fondness. 'I really liked the socks.' She giggled.

The music came on again. Malcolm clung on; his head was still churning, and his stomach had taken on a life of its own. His brain cleared a little, but he held on just a bit longer. Helena pushed him upright, and he stood swaying slightly.

'I was thinking . . .' he shouted above the music, 'I'm going home your way tonight. You live down Woodside Avenue, don't you?' (He hadn't done his research for nothing.)

'Yes,' yelled Helena, puzzled.

'Well, I wondered if, since I was going that way . . .'

'Oh, do you want a lift? I'm going with Robbie in the van. I expect he'll give you a lift. Robbie, can we give Malcolm a lift?'

Malcolm didn't hear the reply, but Robbie looked less than enthusiastic.

'Yeah, well, never mind.' Malcolm gave up gracefully. 'I just wanted to make sure you were all right. I think those two blokes were after you.'

'What two blokes?' queried Helena.

'Them two over there,' said Malcolm. Helena looked where he was pointing. The two men were nowhere to be seen.

Somehow Malcolm staggered back to his seat. Razza was snoring, head back and mouth open. Malcolm reached down to his sock for the bottle. Razza snorted in his sleep. 'Tickles,' he said, and lunged sideways.

'Razza,' said Malcolm urgently, kicking him awake. 'That DJ, what's his name?'

'I dunno, Robbie something, why?'

'Robbie what?'

'Dunno, Green something, Green-hall, Greenhouse, Green-grocer, Greenfly.' Razza giggled. 'Greenfly.'

'Not Pinchin?'

'Pinchin Greenfly,' Razza chuckled happily to himself.

'Pinchin. That's not his name?'

'No, I told you.' Razza was irritable at being disturbed from his dozy haze. 'Greenhouse or something. Pinchin—that's Helena. Helena in biology.'

'I know.'

'Whatsit matter?'

'It doesn't,' said Malcolm sadly. Helena, leaning on the disco unit, was staring dreamily into Robbie's eyes. Malcolm looked at his watch—10.55.

'I'm going.'

The fresh air hit him as he stepped outside. He sang gloomy love songs to himself as he made his unsteady way down the hill.

Then he laughed. Malcolm knew enough to laugh at himself now and again. He remembered the soft warmth of Helena's sweater. The smell: gentle, inviting—body lotion or conditioner or whatever girls used. And her words: 'You're a nut, Malcolm Crouch,' she'd said. Such tenderness, such affection.

OK, he could never beat a rival like Robbie Smarmy Greenfly. Not a sixth former with a van and a disco and no zits. Not yet, but one day. And in the meanwhile they'd be friends, him and Helena Pinchin, and one day she'd realize his true worth.

He hummed a little song to himself and tried a few natty dance steps as he went down the hill. He never turned round to notice the two men following behind.

They were almost on top of him when he got to Broad Oak corner. He stopped there. Suddenly he felt less cheerful. In fact, he felt distinctly queasy.

The two men crept close behind him. Scowler put up an arm to pin him round the neck. Scarface was about to grab his arm. In the nick of time Malcolm jerked forward.

'Uuuuurgh!' His voice rose in a crescendo and was followed by a noise like a bag of peanuts spilling all over the floor. Malcolm was being loudly and dramatically sick. It was the sort that could hit a cat at ten metres. He half turned as he did it, and it wasn't a cat but the legs of Scowler and Scarface that got spattered. Malcolm never saw them—his eyes were closed. Hastily they retreated to the shadows.

Malcolm stood for a moment, trying to remember where he was and why he felt so ill. He had vague memories of bottles in socks, flashing lights and thumping music. His head thumped in time, and he could think of nothing except the joy of lying at home in bed.

He stumbled on again. He'd take the short cut over the railway footbridge. Mum always said it wasn't safe at night, but bed was a lot nearer that way.

He set off up the dark alley that led to the footbridge, and the two men were right behind him. At the top Malcolm paused to watch a train clattering under the bridge. The London train. He glimpsed people reading, drinking coffee, chatting, sleeping. Danchester meant nothing to them, just a blurred set of roofs and chimneys. Lucky them, getting away. Malcolm's head thumped again and he thought of his destination.

The two men had crept past him as he watched. Now they waited, round the bend in the stairs, ready to pounce. Malcolm set off, straight towards their trap. They steeled themselves to grab.

'Hello, young Malcolm,' said a voice behind him. 'Late for a young 'un like you, innit?'

Percy Sedge, Malcolm's next door neighbour, was taking his Pekinese for their nightly walk. Percy was six foot four, and since he'd been made redundant along with Dad, he'd spent every day at the gym pumping iron. Percy would never hurt a fly and was particularly frightened of his pint-sized wife Beryl. Beryl was the reason he spent all day in the gym and half the evening walking the dog. But the thugs crouched in the corner didn't know that. Nonchalantly, they scuttled down the steps and round the corner.

'Not a safe place at night, young Malcolm,' said Percy. 'I'm going home, I'll walk with you. Come on, Maybelline.'

Maybelline was snuffling in a particularly choice corner. Percy, who could never bear to yank her away, stood patiently. Then he and Malcolm set off, side by side. Malcolm did two steps to every one of Percy's. Maybelline did about twenty.

Scarface and Scowler, hidden in some bushes, watched them pass. Silently they fell in behind.

'Goodnight, young Malcolm,' said Percy as they reached home. He stopped to deadhead a marigold. 'Bed for you, young 'un.'

Behind the looped and frilled curtains, they could see Beryl watching telly. 'I think young Maybelline wants another turn round the block.'

Scarface and Scowler watched with impotent rage as the door closed behind Malcolm.

'Never mind,' said Scowler. 'We know where 'e is now. We'll get 'im next time.'

4

SOCCER SUBSTITUTE

Helena turned to Malcolm in biology. 'Did you get home all right on Saturday?' She giggled.

'Yes. Why?'

'You seemed a little bit . . . the worse for wear.'

Mr Parrott paused ominously in his explanation of photosynthesis. Helena turned back.

If you thought I was the worse for wear then, you should have seen me Sunday morning, thought Malcolm.

Where the sunlight touched Helena's hair, it shone in glints of bronze and crimson. Malcolm gazed at it. *So near and yet so far.*

When old 'Sickazza' dived under his desk to get the worksheets, Helena turned to Malcolm again. 'I really liked your waistcoat. Seriously, better than the socks! It's great. Where'd you get it?'

Malcolm explained about Oxfam.

'Oh, I'm not likely to get one like it then, am I? You're really clever at finding things like that. You've got style.'

Malcolm glowed. He felt proud and deeply moved. Helena thought he had style. The bell rang and he hardly stirred. An idea was forming in his head. The conquest of Helena was in sight. He floated out of the biology lab and along the corridor. He touched down when Razza and Jamie Bond tapped him on the shoulder.

'Well done, Malc.' 'Brilliant, mate.' 'They must really like your style.'

What? Had the conquest been made already? Were all the girls after him? He knew they gossiped but even in Broad Heath news didn't spread that quickly.

'Danchester United under-15s. Try-outs Saturday. You're on the list.'

It was true. There on the list—N. Crouch.

Malcolm hovered above the floor once more. Helena liked his style in waistcoats and the man in the flat cap liked his style in mid-field. It was good to feel appreciated.

'Can't you do anything but watch TV?' growled Dad, coming in from the Jobcentre.

That's rich coming from you, thought Malcolm, but he knew better than to say it. He grunted instead.

'And why can't I ever get a proper sentence out of you?' continued Dad.

'Malcolm, take your feet off the sofa,' added Mum, coming in with the tea. 'Any luck?' she asked Dad, sympathy already in her voice. Dad's slumped shoulders had already told her what the answer would be.

'Nothing. They suggest I retrain. I could do bricklaying, hairdressing or keyboard skills. Me! A qualified engineer with twenty-five years experience. No wonder this country's going to the dogs. What is this rubbish anyway?' The last question was addressed to Malcolm.

'It's a video. Genetic Prawn in concert.'

'See what I mean,' continued Dad. 'Youth of today. All stubble and sweat and moth-eaten vests. When I was young we went out in a collar and tie.'

'You must have been the only middle-aged teenager

in the sixties,' observed Stacey, who was doing her nails in the corner.

'No, he wasn't,' said Mum. 'There were quite a few round here. Not exactly Carnaby Street or the Cavern Club in Danchester, you know.'

Mum had been pretty trendy herself. She'd even got married in a mini-dress. Malcolm and Stacey cringed when the photo-album came out. Mum with puffed-up hair, blackened eyes, stiletto heels and a pelmet skirt. Dad behind the wheel of his first Morris Minor. Mum in a kaftan, Dad with wide lapels and flares, Stacey in a pushchair. Mum in a bikini, Dad making sand-castles, Malcolm with ice cream all over his face. Dad never laughed like that now. The last holiday in Beni-dorm was three years ago. The smiles and the tans had long since faded.

Over tea Malcolm tried to cheer Dad up by telling him about the Danchester United try-out.

'Hmmm. Well, you'll never get it, unless you start training properly, my lad. No chance if you don't put the work in. And what about your studies? We'd better see those maths grades improved this term. About time you put some effort into something, young man, instead of lying around watching this . . .'

'Frenetic Shrimp,' offered Mum.

' . . . rubbish,' said Dad, flicking the control back to ITV.

'Who's this prat?' continued Dad as a cheery man in a red jacket explained how a new improved detergent kept his clothes vibrantly clean and smelling great.

'He's that designer bloke from "The Clothes Show",' said Stacey, glancing up.

'Poofter,' said Dad contemptuously. ' "Clothes Show!" What sort of job's that for a bloke—doing needlework?' He flicked the TV off.

Malcolm ate his shepherd's pie in silence. Dad's 'about-time-you-put-some-effort-in' routine was well-worn, but it still managed to be a wind-up. There *was* something Malcolm wanted to put some effort into, but he certainly wasn't telling Dad.

Later that evening, he knocked on Mrs Walenski's door. There was a long pause and an approaching clunk-shuffle before the door creaked open slightly and her wrinkled face appeared in the gap.

'Yes?' She looked puzzled for a moment, then beamed. 'Ah, gardening, waistcoat.'

The door shut while she fumbled with the chain, then opened wide. 'Cuppa tea?' she offered hopefully.

'All right,' said Malcolm. 'I wanted to ask you a favour.'

Over Mrs Walenski's strong sweet tea, he explained his idea.

'It's about waistcoats. I wondered if you could help me. You see, there's this girl I like, I mean, just a bit. She's only a friend . . .'

Mrs Walenski beamed and nodded her understanding.

' . . . and she really likes my waistcoat and so I wondered, if you helped me, whether I could make her one like it. Here, I brought it round. What do you think?'

Mrs Walenski looked at it thoughtfully. She spread her gnarled hands over the subtle shimmering colours. She held it up and peered at the stitching. At last she sat back in the big armchair and looked at Malcolm.

'Yes,' she said. 'We do. You make good. I teach. One day great couturier.'

Malcolm still didn't understand the last word, but he beamed back.

'We do Saturday, yes?'

'Yeah,' said Malcolm. 'Thanks. In the afternoon. I've got an important appointment in the morning.'

Malcolm looked down. Yes, they really were his knobbly knees, his Broad Heath socks, his studded boots stepping—no, striding—onto Danchester United's hallowed pitch. Imaginary cheers echoed round the empty stands.

'You on the list?' The man in the flat cap looked doubtful.

'Er, yeah. M. Crouch.'

Flat-cap consulted his clipboard. 'Says N. Grouch here. OK, over there, just do what the trainer tells you.'

Malcolm took his place and sneaked a glance at twenty other hopefuls. They all looked bigger, fitter and tougher than him. The smarmy git from Landau Boys was there, tossing back his blond hair and flexing his disgustingly tanned muscles.

And then there was no time for looking. There were sit-ups, press-ups, star jumps... on and on for hours until Malcolm was panting and gasping and everyone else looked like they'd just strolled out of the dressing room. Then there was dribbling and passing, tackling and heading. Malcolm's feet had a mind of their own, his head was disconnected to his brain, his boots were made of foam rubber. When the others dribbled their footballs round the last cone he was still halfway. When he came running in to tackle, the ball had disappeared, when he headed it, it landed in the stands.

'Boss,' said the trainer to Flat-cap when they all paused for breath, 'there's twenty-one lads here. Thought you said twenty.'

Flat-cap consulted his clipboard. He read out the list of names. At the end, only one had not answered— Blond Smarmy Git.

45

'Hah!' muttered Malcolm.

'What's your name then?'

'Nigel de Grosch.'

'Ah,' said Flat-cap. 'N. Grouch—I thought there was something funny there.'

Malcolm took his last steps on the hallowed turf. He made his one and only run down into the tunnel. There were no cheers. His cheeks were red with embarrassment.

Alone in the dressing room he untied his boots and watched another dream die. He knew really. If he was honest. Knew he'd never make it, knew big-time football wasn't for him. Yeah, he liked a kick around with the lads. He always would. But all that fitness stuff— he didn't have the heart. All the training in the world and he still wouldn't be good enough. He didn't have the magic. He knew it, and now it was over. Kicking his rucksack as he trudged, he knew he really didn't mind. But Dad though. And Grandad. That was another story.

'How d'you get on then?' demanded Dad as he walked in the door.

'OK.'

'Don't know the results yet, I suppose.'

'Nah, not yet.'

'Hope you did your best.'

'Yeah, Dad, I did my very best.'

Being at home was too uncomfortable. Malcolm went round to Mrs Walenski's.

She was ready and waiting for him. On her large table was a pile of fabrics, and the biscuit tin of cotton reels. Another tin, labelled Bath Oliver Biscuits, was full of embroidery threads—silk, cotton, wool, gold and silver and every colour you could imagine.

A large cardboard box, printed Cusson's Lavender, had 'Patterns—basic blocks' written on it in a hand similar, but less shaky, to the notice on the front door. In it were rows of envelopes labelled 'Jacket—set sleeves', 'Jacket—dolman', 'Skirt—straight, darts', 'Skirt—circular'. Mrs Walenski leaned to the back of it and took out 'Waistcoat—gents, classic'.

'Your girl,' said Mrs Walenski, waving her arms in an hourglass shape, 'what she?'

The meaning was clear. Malcolm blushed. 'Um, I don't know. She's quite small.'

'This?' asked Mrs Walenski, pointing to the corner behind Malcolm. A dressmaker's dummy stood there—a solid womanly figure in padded off-white linen, a bunch of pins stuck in its shoulder.

'Er, smaller, I think. She's about this tall...' Malcolm held his hand level with his eyebrows, '... and this sort of shape.' He glowed crimson as he indicated a shape in the air. 'Quite small.'

'Ah,' said Mrs Walenski, unworried. 'Thi... Thir...' She wrote it down. 32.

'Dunno,' said Malcolm.

'Yes, yes,' said Mrs Walenski. She took some tissue-paper shapes from the envelope and some folded black silk from the pile. She handed Malcolm the big scissors. 'Now we cut,' she said.

They made an odd pair. Malcolm's head, sandy curls on top, shaved at the sides, alongside Mrs Walenski's wispy white. Together they bent over the work. Together they pinned and cut. She showed him how to hold pins in his mouth. He looked worried. She strapped a little pink velvet pincushion to his wrist. He leaned on the tissue paper and tore it. She smacked his arm. He cut crooked. She made him cut straight. She struggled for words. He guessed the right ones.

He traced off the design on his multi-coloured waistcoat front. She found just the right scraps of fabric to copy it. Afternoon drifted into evening and the waistcoat was just beginning to take shape.

'Now, home go,' said Mrs Walenski. 'Take, sew there.'

'Er, no,' said Malcolm. 'Would it be all right if I came back here to sew it?'

'Ah, no machine,' said Mrs Walenski.

'Well, no,' said Malcolm. 'Mum's got a sewing machine. She never uses it, but she's got one. It's just that ... my Dad, he thinks sewing is girl's stuff. Boys ought to be engineers or footballers.'

'Ah, foolish man,' said Mrs Walenski. 'No trouble. You come back. Next Saturday, OK?'

'OK,' agreed Malcolm.

So, next Saturday Malcolm came back and sewed the waistcoat, and next Sunday he could no longer hide his failure with Danchester United.

'Never mind, son, put plenty of practice in and try again. Bit more effort, that's all.'

'No, Dad.'

'What d'you mean, "No, Dad"?'

'I'd never do it. I like football, but not that much.'

'Where's your ambition, boy?' thundered Dad.

'Dunno, not there, I suppose.'

'Why did I get a son like you? Isn't there anything you'd really like to be good at?'

'Dunno, nothing much,' said Malcolm, and was surprised that the image of a multi-coloured waistcoat came into his mind.

'Danchester United too,' said Grandad bleakly. 'And the lad's not bothered. Must be cracked. If bloomin' 'Itler 'adn't gone prancing into Poland ...'

They were sitting in Grandad's little front parlour. It smelt of tobacco and unwashedness. Grandad had been alone for five years since Grandma had passed on and his personal hygiene was a constant source of anxiety to Mum.

Malcolm didn't mind. On the whole, Grandad was his sort of person. You could sit in front of the telly with your feet up at Grandad's. You could eat chocolates and crisps, and baked beans from the tin. You could swear at the ref and tell rude jokes.

But not today. Today was Sunday-tea-at-Grandad's day, when Grandad wore a tie and a cardigan over his shirt and braces and put on old cracked shoes instead of down-at-heel slippers. Mum got out Grandma's best china and Grandad hid his chipped and tea-stained mug in case she scoured it with Jif. Mum threw away a fortnight's pile of cigarette butts, tea-bags and *Daily Mirrors,* collected Grandad's washing in a tightly-knotted plastic bag, and they all sat down to Mr Kipling cakes and salmon sandwiches.

So even Grandad disapproved of him. Malcolm could do no right with anyone these days. Helena hadn't looked at him for two weeks. Whenever he saw her she was hanging round with smarmy zitless Robbie Greenall. Mum was cross because he'd left his football kit in a bag with a wet towel till it all went mouldy and Dad was cross because he'd got an E in maths.

Grandad was grumpy because he was wearing a shirt with a tight collar, and Stacey was grumpy because she wanted to be in the back of Matt's Fiesta in the lay-by on Windybarrow Hill. Dad was grumpy because Dad was always grumpy, and Dad was always grumpy because he didn't have a job.

Malcolm was not at all pleased with life, and even less so when the doorbell rang and Cousin Jeffrey walked in.

'It was kind of you to invite me, Auntie,' said Jeffrey. 'Grandad, great to see you. You're looking well.'

'I can 'ear you, lad,' muttered Grandad. 'No need to shout. Two pints of brown and twenty Players a day. That's what keeps me fit. 'ealthier than all that religion of yours.'

Rubbish, thought Malcolm. *Grandad doesn't look at all well. He looks like the thing the dog chews, or the thing that walked out in 'The Curse of the Mummy's Tomb'.*

'And Malcolm, I am glad you're here. I've been wanting to see you. I've got this great event coming up I think you'll be interested in.'

'Oh Jeffrey, I am sorry. I'm busy every Saturday now, what with football and er, studying and all.'

'No, it's not Saturdays. It's a whole week—in August. An adventure camp in Scotland, just the sort of thing you'd like.'

'Wanna bet?' muttered Malcolm.

'Oh Malcolm, that sounds like a nice idea,' said Mum.

'Yeah, but Mum, think of the money.'

'It's really cheap,' said Jeffrey, 'It's subsidized. By the Ethel Howe Youth Temperance Fund.'

'Yeah, but we can't afford anything, can we? Dad said . . .'

'Come on, Malcolm, we're not down on our uppers yet,' said Dad jovially.

'But you said . . .'

Dad had the sort of fixed smile that says, *Shut up or I'll kill you.*

'Oh, I've got a little bit put by,' said Mum hastily. 'I think we might manage.'

'What d'they do on this adventure thingy?' asked Grandad.

'Oh, mountain stuff: rock-climbing, hiking . . .'

'Make a man of you, lad,' said Grandad.

'... And water sports: canoeing, sailing.'

'Bet you like that then, Jeffrey,' giggled Stacey. This was a reference to a family outing to Billstone Ponds, when Jeffrey had been seasick on a pedalo.

Jeffrey ignored her. 'Yes, Grandad, that's the idea. Character building.'

'Better go yourself then, lad,' said Grandad sourly.

Jeffrey ignored him. 'What d'you think then, Malcolm?'

I think I'd rather be hung by the feet over a pit of anacondas, thought Malcolm.

'Thanks for asking, I'll give it some thought,' he said. And to himself he added, *And the most thought will go into how to get out of it.*

5

SHADOWY FIGURES

Malcolm was still thinking about how to get out of Jeffrey's holiday when they arrived home. To their surprise the front door stood open.

'Who was last out?' asked Mum. 'Malcolm, was it you?'

But as they crossed the threshold all thoughts of excuses and blame were forgotten. The place had been turned upside down. There was a dusty patch where the TV and video once stood. Drawers and cupboards were opened, their contents tipped out.

Malcolm's room was the worst. Everything had been pulled out and onto the floor. Now the floor, of course, was where most things lived in Malcolm's room, but this was turmoil on a different scale. Every cupboard, every drawer, every box emptied. Clothes, tapes, Lego, Masters of the Universe toys that he'd never quite got rid of, his road signs, his collection of beer bottles—everything was thrown about the room. But there didn't seem to be anything missing. His stereo and his computer, the most valuable things he possessed, were still on the shelf.

The policemen scratched their heads. 'Well, it seems they were looking for something—but whatever it was, they didn't find it. You're sure nothing else has gone?'

'No, just the TV and the video,' said Mum. 'They must have seen my gold bracelet and Aunt Amy's ring, but they didn't take them.'

'They left my CD player,' added Stacey.

'Well, we'll fingerprint, but the chances of catching the blighters are almost nil, I'm afraid. Are you insured?'

'Oh yes,' said Mum.

Dad shifted a little in his chair.

Dad slumped in front of the place where the TV once stood. Mum sat at the table and dried her eyes. The shouting had finished now, but Malcolm had heard it all from the bedroom.

'What d'you mean, you forgot?'

'I forgot, that's all.'

'You've got nothing else to do, for goodness sake.'

'Oh yes, hit where it hurts. That's hardly my fault.'

'I ask you to do one thing, just one thing, instead of sitting round on your backside all day, and you forget to do it.'

Silence.

'Well, you won't be able to sit on your backside all day now. Or if you do, you'll just have to stare at the wall.'

Dad had 'forgotten' to renew the insurance.

'Money was so tight,' he admitted eventually. 'I thought it was something that could wait. I was expecting that benefit money, remember?'

'Oh yes, the benefit they decided we weren't entitled to.'

'It was only so we had enough for Christmas presents. I didn't want people saying my kids were going short. I was going to pay it eventually.'

So there was to be no money for a new TV. No new video. And there was worse to come.

'I cannot believe you would keep that much money in an envelope behind the clock.' This was Dad accusing now.

'It was just odd bits I'd saved.'

'But that's what banks are for, you pea-brained woman.'

'At least I tried to save. I didn't want anything grand, just a caravan or something.'

'Fat chance now.'

Mum had been putting money away for a family holiday. £275 tucked behind the clock. That too had gone.

Gloom descended on the Crouch household like a thick polluting smog.

Malcolm went round to Mrs Walenski's more and more. He cut her grass and mended her fence and in exchange she let him watch her television and helped him make the waistcoat. Carefully she guided him through each process in copying the shimmering rainbow fronts. First paint on the background satin in deepening shades of bluey-green. Then add the rainbow in machine embroidery stitches—thick rows of satin stitch subtly uneven so that the colours blended. It was hard work—whoever had designed the original waistcoat was no beginner. Malcolm had to practise over and over—trying again and again until the effect was just right.

'Oi, oi, see, see. This boy good,' proclaimed Mrs Walenski. 'One day you ma ... ma ...'

'Man?' tried Malcolm. 'Mad? Magic?'

'Magic,' repeated Mrs Walenski. 'Magic.'

Then the hand embroidery. Lines of gold and silver threading through the rainbow. Minute glass beads dotted like drops of water. It was painful for Mrs Walenski to hold the needle and demonstrate, but she was determined to try.

Malcolm thought sewing by hand would be boring, but he found to his surprise he quite liked it. It was peaceful sitting there stitching away. Easier to forget his problems.

'What is a stroke?' he asked Mrs Walenski one day as he sat stitching raindrops. He had discovered that with a combination of mime, word guessing games and writing down she could explain most things. As long as you weren't in a hurry.

There was no hurrying her now. She stood up and took her walking frame, shuffle-clunk, shuffle-clunk, over to the bookcase. Mrs Walenski liked books. She bought them, like she bought most things, from mail-order catalogues. She liked illustrated ones most, and illustrated gardening books best of all. She used her pincers to pull down a book from the top shelf—a medical dictionary.

'Cerebral thrombosis' said the book, *'common name: stroke. Paralysis may occur and speech may be affected. Often partial or full recovery may occur. Intelligence is not affected, but the ability to translate ideas into words may be lost.'*

'So it's like everything's in there, in your head, but you just can't get the words out?' asked Malcolm.

Mrs Walenski nodded. She clenched her fists and screwed up her face. 'Eeeeeeow,' she said as a way of explaining how frustrating it was.

'I bet,' said Malcolm. 'And have you really got plastic knees?'

If Mrs Walenski wasn't batty, then perhaps it was true. She turned to the front of the dictionary.

'Arthritis: painful inflammation of the joints . . . In extreme circumstances hip or knee replacements may reduce pain and improve mobility.'

'Woh! Have you got plastic hips too?'

'One,' agreed Mrs Walenski, pointing.

'That's neat, isn't it? Plastic hips, dead clever.' Malcolm considered it. 'So have you been in hospital millions of times?'

Mrs Walenski considered. 'Millions.'

She thumbed through her notebook. It was an address book really but in it she kept all sorts of useful information. There at the back was a list:

Arthritis 1975
Strokes 1983, 1987
Operations 1980, 1985, 1991.

'Does it still hurt, the arthritis?' Malcolm's curiosity had overcome his politeness.

'Every day, every night.'

'What, every day since 1975?'

Mrs Walenski nodded. Then she rapped his fingers with a ruler. 'Bad boy. Keep sewing. I get cuppa tea.'

'Twenty years,' thought Malcolm on the way home. 'Twenty years of hurting every day and she's still smiling. If she can do it . . .'

But being happy in the Crouch household stood out like a nun at a rave.

'What've you got to be so bloomin' cheerful about?' asked Dad. 'Especially after your last report.'

'Are you taking the mick?' asked Stacey, when Malcolm told her how nice she looked.

'If you've got that much energy, come and wash up,' said Mum.

Malcolm gave up.

Some people, however, never give up. Jeffrey arrived one day brimming with Christian cheer.

'You know, Auntie, "all things work together for them that love God". "Joy cometh in the morning," you know.'

'I don't think this house is on her rounds, lad,' said Dad dourly.

Jeffrey just went on. 'The thing is, "the Lord moves in mysterious ways"...'

'He certainly hasn't explained himself round here,' said Dad.

'... and I've just been told there's a free place on this adventure holiday for children from reduced circumstances.'

Dad sat up straight and gripped the chair till his knuckles whitened.

Great, Jeffrey—about as much tact as a strippergram in a funeral parlour, thought Malcolm.

'... and I thought it would be ideal for Malcolm. Now you've got no telly, he must be bored.'

Brilliant one, Jeffrey, right below the belt.

'... It really is an excellent holiday, Malcolm, and it would get you out of the house.'

Malcolm looked round the room. He met Mum's red-rimmed, grey-bagged eyes. Dad stared at the wall, but his knuckles were still white.

As if on cue, Stacey yelled from upstairs. 'Malcolm, have you been in my room? What have you done with my shower gel?'

'I haven't touched your rotten...' began Malcolm and then stopped. Nothing could be worse than this. 'OK, Jeffrey, I'll come.'

A Friday evening at the end of the summer term. Rosy clouds over the tortilla factory, rooks cawing in the distant trees, and in the corner of the empty rec., a small clump of boys hanging around the swings.

Malcolm moved to the roundabout. He gave it a good push and jumped on. He lay on his back on the wooden slats, his head hanging out. He watched the world circling upside down—trees, houses, clouds, factory, sunset, trees, houses . . .

'But how do you know it'll be religious?' asked Razza, twisting his swing round and round until the chains clanked.

'It will. I know Jeffrey, he thinks my soul needs saving.'

'Have you got one?' asked Marty, standing on his swing and swaying slowly like the metronome in music class.

'Dunno,' said Malcolm, leaning back and gazing at his shadow, lengthening and disappearing by turns.

'You don't believe in all this God stuff, do you?' asked Jamie, giving the roundabout another push.

Malcolm looked dizzily up at the circling sky. Gold going to rose-red turning to hazy blue merging with purple grey.

'Well,' he ventured. 'There must be someone out there.'

The others surveyed the evening calm.

'Guess so,' said Marty, after a pause.

'There is,' said Razza suddenly. 'Over there, I just seen them.'

'What, God?' asked Jamie.

'Nah, in the bushes, look, there's someone there.'

They peered at the rustling bushes. Two pairs of eyes peered back at them, then disappeared. There was a stillness, then two men strolled casually out and away to the park entrance.

'It's those blokes,' said Razza. 'They were hanging about outside your house earlier, Malc.'

'Yeah, I've seen them before,' agreed Marty.

'Weren't they at the school disco?' asked Si Parker, lying upside down on the slide.

The sky darkened to rich ink. The moon sliced a

thin arc in the darkness and here and there stars pierced the gloom. The roundabout had stopped. Malcolm lay still till his head stopped too. He looked at his watch.

'Gotta go.'

'What, now?'

'Yeah, I'm catching the night coach up to Scotland. Jeffrey and me are picking it up at the by-pass. Have a good holiday, fellas.'

'Oh, come on,' said Razza to the others. 'We'll walk home with you.'

Malcolm picked up his bag, ready packed, at home. On the spur of the moment he pulled out his Oxfam waistcoat. The new-made waistcoat remained at Mrs Walenski's—just a few finishing stitches to be made. But he'd reclaimed the original and he put it on now. It was a kind of statement: *I'm not going to turn into a Bible-basher. Take me the way I am.*

Mum fussed and Dad managed an 'Enjoy yourself, son,' without looking up from his chair. The clock moved round to 10.30 and Jeffrey didn't arrive.

'Perhaps he can't make it,' suggested Malcolm, hopefully.

But then the phone rang. 'The prayer meeting overran. I'll meet you at the by-pass.'

Malcolm hoisted his holdall on to his shoulder and put his baseball cap on backwards.

'See you then,' and he stepped out into the dark.

He didn't notice the two figures fall into step behind him. Once he thought he heard footsteps and stopped. The footsteps stopped too, or maybe he'd imagined them. A police car cruised past, a gang of little kids called him names, a couple snogging at the bus stop looked up as he passed.

He plodded past the parade of shops, dark and shuttered except for the two at the end. The off-licence and the chip shop—high spot of Broad Heath's night life. They were busy now as Malcolm approached. A crowd came out of the chip shop and piled into a van—Robbie Greenall's van. Malcolm could have sworn that was Helena among them.

Depression chilled him to his toes. The street fell suddenly silent and he stopped, digging in his pocket for change. Behind him two figures crept ever nearer. A gaggle of giggly girls came out of the off-licence. 'Hello, Malcolm,' called one. They went off singing 'Jingle Bells' and sniggering loudly.

Malcolm stomped into the fish and chip shop. 'Bag of chips please, and a pickled onion. Oh, and a bottle of Irn Bru.' Malcolm counted out his pennies and two shadowy figures peered in through the glass.

Cheered by the hot chips, Malcolm plodded on to the by-pass. The road was deserted now and one solitary street lamp burned. Down on the by-pass the traffic whizzed by, but here on the slip road all was dark and silent. Malcolm stared at the empty road and round the corner two dark, silent figures stared at him. One of them took a knife from his pocket and flicked it open. The other held a scarf ready as a gag. A lorry swung round, lighting up the corner and they shrunk back. Malcolm paced up and down. He turned and paced towards them. Again they hid in the shadows. He reached the nearest point and turned. They stepped out, ready to pounce.

'Hello there, pleasant evening, isn't it? If you can spare a minute or two, I have a booklet here I think might interest you.'

Scowler and Scarface looked in blank amazement at the figure before them. It was the Hunchback of Notre

Dame turned super salesman. In the dim light they could see only the proffered booklet, a wide sincere smile and slogans gleaming on the head and chest. He stepped forward into the faint lamplight and Quasimodo turned into Jeffrey, a huge rucksack on his back. 'Jesus rules OK' proclaimed his cap. 'I've got the answer, what's your question?' was emblazoned across his chest.

'It's a copy of Mark's Gospel,' continued Jeffrey hopefully. 'Have you ever wondered about the root of evil in society today?'

The two men stared at him wildly. Scowler slid the knife away, like a naughty child caught playing with a dangerous toy.

From around his corner, Malcolm couldn't see who Jeffrey was talking to. He only knew that his cousin was a Grade A Super-Nerd to be disowned at all costs.

A growling burst of light came up from the by-pass. It was the coach.

'There's a leaflet enclosed giving service times at Danchester New Life Fellowship. A warm welcome awaits . . .' Jeffrey was calling as he climbed aboard behind Malcolm. The driver swore as Jeffrey's rucksack hit him in the eye.

'You know, Malcolm, I think the Lord really spoke to those fellows. I really felt they were burdened under the guilt of sin.'

Malcolm stared gloomily out of the window. The dark night was slashed by headlights racing south.

'God moves in mysterious ways,' continued Jeffrey. 'I really think my coming along just then was all part of his plan.'

'If that stupid bloke hadn't come along,' said Scowler.
'I told you, we should have followed the coach,' said Scarface.

'How? Jogging along the motorway? I told you we shouldn't have left the car.'

'Well, we know they're going to Scotland.'

'Scotland's a big place.'

'Yeah . . .'

'And a long way.'

'So?'

'So we haven't got enough petrol. And we're broke, remember—till we do the job and get paid.'

'Broke!' Scarface looked disgusted. 'We're criminals, aren't we? If you 'aven't got it, nick it.'

'Oh yeah.' Scowler screwed his face in thought. 'Well, it's too late now. I've got enough for a can of beer.'

Georgie Climes flinched when the two men grabbed his arms. He'd been nicking chocolate bars in the off-licence.

'You look like our sort of fella,' said Scarface with a menacing smile. They took him by the elbows and led him out.

'Oi, I'll tell the Bill on you,' screeched Georgie. 'Child abuse, that's what. I'm only eleven.' A thought struck. 'You're not the Bill, are you?'

They laughed. 'Wanna do a job for us?'

Georgie nodded nervously.

'D'you know a kid in a fancy waistcoat? Bit bigger than you. He was round here earlier.'

'Yeah, gingery hair, curly on top. Dunno his name.'

'That's the one. He's gone away for a bit, but here's his address, be back in a week or two, I should think. Could you keep an eye out for him. Give us a ring if he turns up. He's a friend of ours, see.'

Georgie eyed them carefully. 'What's in it for me?'

'Fiver.'

'Up-front.'

'Ah, well, yeah, cash flow problem.'

'Tenner then, as soon as I phone.'

'You're on. Here's the number. Any time. We wanna get in touch with him, see. Don' tell him though. We want it to be a surprise.'

6

MOUNTAIN BIKER

Dear Mrs Walenski
The good news is—the mountains are fantastic.
The bad news is—it rains all the time.
The bad news is—there are no girls.
The good news is—the blokes are pretty cool.
See you when I get back.
Malcolm

On Monday evenings they sat you down to write postcards home. Mum and Dad's said the usual minimum: 'Got here OK, camp OK, food OK, weather lousy', but Malcolm surprised himself by writing to Mrs Walenski. Postcards meant a lot to her. She would show you her latest with great pride regardless of whether you knew Maisie at Great Yarmouth or Laurence and Jane in Venice. You'd think that someone who never went anywhere would be jealous of the travels of others, but when those gaudy colour prints with their trivial messages dropped through the letter box, they made Mrs Walenski's day.

So Malcolm sent a postcard to Mrs Walenski. He also surprised himself by what he wrote. 'The blokes are pretty cool.' And they were. This was the second discovery—the first was that Jeffrey had forgotten to tell him it was a boys-only camp—that not all religious types were as nerdy as Jeffrey. They were really quite normal—a good laugh. They liked Leadbitter Riff and Genetic Prawn and supported decent teams like Arsenal, Liverpool and Villa. They did all the usual things like spraying shaving foam on midnight raids, and putting clingfilm over loos and spiders in sleeping-bags. They even added a few new refinements like parcel-taping one of the leaders to his chair, then carrying him out and hanging him over a waterfall. Malcolm had to admit that showed an unusual degree of class. He hoped they'd try Jeffrey next.

The camp was like another world—little log cabins dotted among pine trees on a high mountain plateau. Around it the peaks rose grey and mysterious. A brown peaty stream wandered through the trees and above it a splendidly hairy-scary assault course. To get to the camp you drove for ever up a narrow winding lane, and in between high wooden fences like a Wild West stockade. Craigmor Mountain Adventure Centre it said above the gateway. Inside, as well as the bunk rooms there was a huge barn-like games room with table tennis, snooker, badminton and darts. There was even a TV room. Set out on the ridge was the meeting cabin; easy chairs ranged round a large brick fireplace. They lit the log fire, even in August. It was welcome on rainy nights.

Apparently this religious crowd—Malcolm nicknamed them the Commitments—came here once a year. 'We must be a blessing to them,' Jeffrey explained solemnly. 'All the rest of the time they take young offenders—thugs and thieves and people who *drink*.'

Findlay, the Centre Leader, looked well able to deal with thugs and thieves. He was a man of few words, huge and scruffy, bearded, earringed and pigtailed, with stained jeans that hung just a little below a check-shirted belly. Malcolm doubted that Big Fin—as he was universally known—was so very blessed by this week's guests. Certainly he steered well clear of the evening meetings, choosing to busy himself coiling ropes, sorting life-jackets or chopping logs. When he'd finished for the night he would sit quietly by the stream with a cigarette and a bottle of beer. Malcolm wished he could join him.

Meetings! The religious bit. That was the only problem. You all sat round singing happy-clappy songs to an out-of-tune guitar and then someone came and preached at you. At this point, people who'd been a good laugh all day suddenly became serious, or joyful, or worst of all seriously joyful. The songs all told God how wonderful he was and how joyful you were at how wonderful he was and how wonderful it was that you were so joyful about how wonderful he was. You did this about thirty times over.

Still, thought Malcolm, *it's better than the po-faced hymns at Scout parade.* They were all about being a sinful pilgrim through a barren land with eventide falling fast. You only sang them once through. God needed reminding how weak and feeble you were, but it wouldn't do to pester him.

The funny thing was that at camp after all this joyful stuff, someone got up to speak and still told you what a feeble sinner you were. They didn't talk in churchy voices and they did talk about ordinary things like TV programmes and football and going on dates. They even cracked a few jokes. But still they all ended the same way. 'You need God. Jesus can change you.'

Malcolm didn't understand this Jesus stuff. Not understanding made him irritable and he got especially mad when the talk invariably ended with an 'Is Jesus speaking to you? Respond to him now . . .' routine. Malcolm had this nasty feeling that everyone was looking at him. He was certain Jeffrey was. Jeffrey had a technique which brought the cringe factor to red hot embarrassment. At first, during the final song, he would just look at Malcolm hopefully. Malcolm pretended not to notice. Then Jeffrey would sink to his chair and bury his head in his hands in an attitude of fervent prayer. At about the fifth repetition of the song, they stopped and the bloke did the 'I'm sure there's someone here the Lord is speaking to . . .' bit. Then Jeffrey would peek through his fingers to see what Malcolm was doing. On the third day Malcolm stopped pretending, and made a very rude sign with his fingers.

After the meeting Jeffrey told Malcolm that he had no spiritual sensitivity and that bringing him along was like casting pearls before swine. Malcolm just grunted.

But the rest was OK. He learnt how to get roped up and climb a rock face. Admittedly it was a fairly tame little rock face, but all the same he discovered how to find finger-holds and toe-holds in an impossibly sheer slab of granite. He learnt how to paddle a canoe in a straight line instead of round and round in circles, and how to turn it over and come up the other side. Malcolm was quite chuffed to discover he could do these sorts of things, even if he did feel scared spitless at first.

For all his threatening exterior, Big Fin was great at making you feel safe. He supervised all the activities, demonstrating what to do in a laid-back, off-hand manner and answering questions with a single word. But he was always alert. Nothing got past his gaze. If a boy was muddled or scared, Big Fin was there with a quiet explanation or word of encouragement. And the beer gut was deceptive. Big Fin was strong. If you were about to fall, Findlay's arm was there, catching you, hauling you in.

The only thing that got Big Fin going was a show-off. For them he had a few choice words. Once was enough for most people to get the wrong end of Big Fin's tongue. You had to be thick-skinned or an incurable show-off to get it twice. Colin Bell was both of those things.

Colin was the only person Malcolm didn't like. Colin was posh. Colin had been everywhere, done everything, got everything. Malcolm had stopped going anywhere or getting anything much when Dad lost his job, so Colin's boasting got right up his nose. When Colin went on about white-water rafting on the Colorado River, Malcolm made a rather loud comment about people who couldn't stop their canoe going aground, and when Colin went on about his Muddy Fox mountain bike, Malcolm agreed that it would have to be tough to take Colin's weight. Colin just sneered about people who were only jealous.

On the fourth night the subject for the evening talk was Ambition. The speaker seemed to think that God wanted you to be ambitious. 'Trust in the Lord and he will give you the desires of your heart,' he quoted. This was a new one on Malcolm; a bit different from Jeffrey's 'if you enjoy it, it must be wrong' school of religion. 'What is it you most want for your life?' went on the speaker. 'What do you most want to be?'

Malcolm thought about it. Definitely not a gardener. Not an engineer. Sadly, not a footballer. A rock musician would be good, but he'd have to learn to play an instrument first, and how to sing in tune. A computer game inventor? Computers were all right but . . . No, what he really wanted was . . .

What he really wanted to be was a fashion designer. He wanted to make clothes. It was odd, but it was true.

He knew. He just knew. In Mrs Walenski's satins, silks and sewing machine, he had found something that excited him more than anything else.

'God wants to fulfil your dreams,' declaimed the speaker. 'He wants you to give your ambitions to him.' His voice rose dramatically. 'Give them to him now.'

'What I'm going to suggest you do,' said the speaker, going down a gear into normal speech, 'is to write down your ambition on a piece of paper. Then we're going to collect them up and offer them all to God in prayer.'

Malcolm wasn't sure about prayer, but he did it all the same. *Just imagine if there really was someone out there. I s'pose if he made me he must know what I like. S'pose he wanted me to do what I like.* He wrote down 'Fashion Designer'. It was a promise to himself. He folded it and put it in the basket they passed round. But he passed it to Colin and the fold sprang open. Malcolm saw him read it and glance up with a smirk.

After the meeting, over hot chocolate and flapjacks, Colin pounced. He held up a limp wrist, prancing up to Malcolm as if on a catwalk. Malcolm was wearing ex-army trousers with Grandad's old braces. Colin pinged the braces. 'D'you know, I thought you just couldn't afford new clothes. I didn't know it was a fashion statement. Designer, eh? Goin' to make pretty frocks, are you? No wonder you don't get on with us tough outdoor types.'

Malcolm grunted. Grunting was safe. It was his standard defence against everything the world threw at him. But inside... oh, inside he seethed and boiled and raged, and hoped Colin would ride his Muddy Fox into a Volvo. He pictured it mangled under the wheels. He visualized Colin's bloodied teeth scattered over the tarmac. He saw him trapped upside down in a canoe with piranha fish closing in; dangling over a precipice while a goat chewed the rope; parcel-taped to the London to Aberdeen railway line and the express on the way. That night Malcolm went off to sleep devising tortures for Colin.

It didn't stop the hurt.

It wasn't just Colin. Colin was a big-mouthed nerd, but it was more than that. Malcolm never put it in words, but it was as if he'd taken a tiny unsure step towards someone out there, and someone out there had kicked him back.

The next morning was mountain biking. Boys and bikes were taken by Land Rover to the cloud-covered slopes of Ben Carroch. Then each boy was set off at five-minute intervals down the narrow mountain track.

'The track's marked with yellow arrows,' explained Findlay, 'one at every bend and every fork. Do not under any circumstances go off the track. Keep it steady. Don't brake suddenly. Not unless you want to rearrange your face in a lump of granite. Safety, not speed. This isn't a race.'

But unofficially it was. 'Last year I was 2 minutes 29 seconds faster than anyone else,' said Colin to anyone who would listen. Malcolm pretended not to.

Waiting for his turn on the misty mountain top and getting cold and bored, Malcolm strolled over to the Land Rover. Big Fin's Ordnance Survey map lay open in the back. Malcolm was OK at maps, he'd done them in Scouts. The track down from the top was obvious enough, Hamish had marked it in blue biro. You could see how it snaked its way back and forth down the steep contour lines.

There was another track, Malcolm noticed, cutting off huge loops of the main one and going almost directly down. He studied it carefully, a plan half-forming in his mind.

Colin went before him, complaining about the inferiority of this bike compared to his own at home.

'Never mind, Colin, skill will always show itself,' said Malcolm. Colin looked hard to see if this was a wind-up, but decided it was a compliment. He smiled graciously as he set off down the gravelly track between the heather.

And now it was Malcolm's turn. He fastened his helmet and pushed off. He didn't ride a bike now, not since he'd grown out of his BMX, but he used to be good—the best. The mist hid the view. He knew they were high up, but you could see nothing and no one below. It muffled the sound too. You were alone with your whirring machine in a secret grey world. Every so often a yellow arrow would come at you through the mist, warning you of the next bend. Malcolm slowed as he approached the third one. There, sure enough, a narrow track veered off, descending more steeply through the bleak moorland.

Malcolm ignored the yellow arrow.

The path plunged down, steep but not too steep. *This is a cinch*, thought Malcolm. He imagined Colin's face when he found Malcolm ahead of him.

The mist was a worry. *Surely I should be joining the main path by now*, thought Malcolm as he hurtled ever onwards and downwards. The landscape changed. Boulders began to appear among the heather. Rivulets started to flow down the track, others joined them and made it a stream. Malcolm noticed clumps of thick, reedy grass. The firm ground beneath the wheels turned to mud. The bike slowed, squelched, then stopped.

Uh huh, so much for that idea, thought Malcolm. He dismounted and lifted the bike to his shoulders. Puffing and panting he picked his way through the bog, trying to find the firm ground. He was not successful. Mud oozed over his socks and boggy water seeped into his trainers. He tried to the left, then the right. He had gone several metres around the mountainside before he found a solid mound of rock. Gratefully he climbed on to it.

And there was the track, meandering just below on the other side. No one was on it.

Hah, I might still beat him, thought Malcolm. He scrambled down the slope and mounted his bike once more. He thought he could hear the whirring of a cycle behind him, but he didn't stop to look.

Yes, this is definitely the right track, thought Malcolm. It was winding down in just the way he expected, coming below the moorland now and into the forest. The pine trees were dark and silent. Only the cracking of twigs under his wheels showed anything was alive here.

'Pilgrim through this barren land,' hummed Malcolm as he cycled on. The track took a turn but there was no yellow arrow. *Funny,* thought Malcolm. *Still, I'm sure it's right.*

The track emerged from the forest, no heather this time, just threadbare grass and a few desolate trees. The mist was lifting, so Malcolm could see what was ahead of him. And what was ahead of him was—nothing!

The track turned sharply. It just kept turning, but Malcolm didn't. He braked sharply and the bike skidded on the bare soil. It wouldn't stop. Malcolm saw it all in slow motion—boy and bike heading relentlessly towards a sheer precipice. The branch above him and his hands grabbing the branch. The bike hurtling over into nothingness while Malcolm clung, horrified, to the branch.

He heard it in slow motion too. A sort of whoosh as the bike went through the air, twanging crashes as it bounced off the rocks and a dull thud as it landed. Then a crack as the branch broke and landed him painfully on wet gravel. A bird flying up with a cawking cry and a whirring of wings. Then silence.

Deep horrible silence as Malcolm picked himself up and rubbed the dirt from his grazed hands. He staggered up. Blood was seeping through the knees of his jeans. He stood for a moment before doing what he had to do—peering over the edge. It must have been a quarry of some sort, though worked no longer. He was looking down a sheer overhanging drop of some forty or fifty metres. At the bottom was a jagged clump of rocks and beyond that, sealing off the base of the cliff, a deep, silent pool. Half-way down the cliff, the bike was lodged, caught in a clump of spiky bushes. It hung there, buckled and bent, one wheel still slowly spinning. Malcolm imagined, though he tried not to, himself hanging there. Or worse, hurtling the full depth of the chasm to the sharp rocks below. He felt sick, dizzy and extremely foolish.

'Did no one see him?' asked Big Fin.

'I was next down, and I didn't,' said one.

'D'you think he had a puncture?' asked another helpfully.

'P'raps he's scared of heights,' offered someone.

Malcolm wished the ground would swallow him up. It refused to do so. Somehow he had managed to stagger down the path, and somehow it had ended up right at the place where a knot of boys and bikes stood around the Land Rover. They all looked back up the other track, the right track. Malcolm wondered if he could just sneak off and catch a coach back to London. Then someone turned.

'Fin, Fin, there he is.'

Malcolm shuffled out of the undergrowth. Big Fin watched silently as he approached, calmly taking in boggy feet, bleeding knees and an obvious lack of bike.

'Well?' said Big Fin ominously.

The explanation made Big Fin's brow furrow and everyone else snigger a little. The sniggering died away when Malcolm explained where the bike was. Big Fin's face turned to thunder.

'You bleedin' blitherin' idiot. Thought you were so clever, didn't you? Thought you knew a better way— you, who've never set foot there. Smart-alec boy scouts give me the pip. You've just written off £300-worth of bike. Not to mention the fact that you could be dead. Dead, boy, dead. Lying there stiff at the bottom of a quarry. Dead clever, that.'

Malcolm felt all too alive, rattling along in the back of the Land Rover, all too aware of bruised legs, stinging hands and burning cheeks. All too alive to the fact that £300-worth of bike was hanging ruined halfway down a cliff, and someone was going to have to pay for it. Malcolm had a horrid feeling he knew who that someone was. All he could see as the Land Rover raced through the spectacular scenery was Dad's face. And Dad's face was very, very angry.

'Malcolm Crouch,' called Big Fin as they got out of the Land Rover. 'Go and get cleaned up. You'll need a hot bath. Here, antiseptic—make sure it's on every cut and graze.' He turned away to the roof rack.

'But . . .' said Malcolm.

'We'll deal with the rest later,' said Findlay, starting to unstrap the bikes.

7

GOOD SAMARITAN

But the next day Malcolm heard nothing about it. It was Wednesday and Wednesdays at the Adventure Centre were set aside for conquering the Talloch Ridge. No rock faces to climb, but a steep slog up to Ben Garmon, the highest peak in the area, and then along the ridge and down past Loch Brenna, 25 kilometres in all. The whole camp did this together. Even Jeffrey, who'd 'felt called' to stay behind and peel vegetables most days, couldn't get out of this one.

He appeared at breakfast clad in grim determination and what he considered a suitable outfit for mountains. Cousin Julia and her husband Paul went skiing once a year and Jeffrey had borrowed Paul's ski-wear. The lime green lycra body suit looked a trifle odd on Jeffrey's lanky frame, especially with the Adventure Centre's hired boots and red socks at the bottom of it. But it was the quilted jacket, like a huge yellow puffball, that really made the difference. He looked like a rather worried overgrown dandelion, and Malcolm hoped everyone else had forgotten they were related.

There is something soothing about climbing a mountain. Your body takes on a rhythm—left, right, left, right—and all your energy is absorbed in the steady plod upwards. And as you rise higher you seem to leave your troubles behind. The world spread out below you is so vast, so beautiful, that all the things that worry you are somehow less important.

That was how Malcolm felt anyway, as he sat on the summit of Ben Garmon and watched the sunshine and shadows racing over the purple and green landscape below. The wind cooled his face like a crystal stream, and his cheese and pickle sandwiches, crisps, chocolate bar and apple were like a banquet from the gods.

Below the belt, however, Malcolm felt less heavenly. He had eaten an awful lot of baked beans over the last few days. Maybe that was the problem. Whatever the reason, there were strange stirrings in his bowels, and he was beginning to get worried. There were no loos on this mountain, and not a bush in sight.

'OK, fellas,' said Big Fin. 'Time to move on.'

Good timing. A malevolent cloud chose this moment to come down, hovering about the mountain top and suddenly shrouding them in mist. Malcolm shivered.

Jeffrey drew a long green woolly hat from one pocket of his puffball and stuffed his tracts in the other. They'd passed several groups of hikers, trekking miles to escape the pressures of civilization, and each of them had been pestered with one of Jeffrey's leaflets.

'Perhaps they think he's an alien,' thought Malcolm. The long green hat gave him the appearance of a tall spindly Klingon. Malcolm kept well away from him.

Plodding down in the mist is not as much fun as plodding up in the sunshine—especially when you know you're only going down in order to go up again. They were descending into Dead Man's Gully before climbing up again to the Talloch Ridge. Malcolm's interior rumblings were beginning to take over. He tried to fight a rising tide of panic.

Another group of walkers passed them. 'Excuse me,'

asked Malcolm, quietly detaching himself from the rest of the party, 'did you pass any toilets on the way down here?'

They looked puzzled, and muttered a string of gobbledegook words.

'Toilet, loo, lavatory,' repeated Malcolm. He performed a mime worthy of Mrs Walenski.

'*Ach, Toiletten*,' said one. '*Nein*.' The Germans shook their heads and went off laughing.

'They must have lavatory jokes in German too,' thought Malcolm.

But it was no joke. He had dropped back from his group of friends now and the next group was several metres behind. Malcolm was getting desperate. He looked wildly round. The barren landscape afforded not a scrap of cover—just vast stretches of rough grass or ankle-deep heather.

What was that over there? A sheep, munching the grass, abruptly went over a hillock and disappeared. A hiding place! A loo! It was a few hundred metres away, but he could always catch up. Caring nothing for what anyone thought and clutching at the tissues in his pocket, he dashed over the hillock to the point the sheep disappeared.

He found himself in a narrow rocky gully, presumably the home of the Dead Man. If he ducked down, he was almost hidden from view. There was no time to be lost. The sheep eyeballed him balefully, conveying, Malcolm felt, a deep sense of outrage.

'Look, sheep,' said Malcolm apologetically. 'I'm sorry if this is your patch and all, but there's a lot of other mountain out there for you. I need this bit. It's urgent. Anyway, it's biodegradable.'

The sheep trotted off in disgust. Malcolm understood its point of view, but could feel only immense relief. From his position, crouched in the gully, he could see the whole Adventure Centre party pass by. Far in the distance, Findlay, at the head of the party, had turned left and up the hill. They all followed, fifty or so teenage boys, straggling along in groups of five or six. Last of all, he saw old Tom Bolt, khaki shorts and Camp Leader since the prehistoric age. They let him come now as a sort of honorary leader. He was supposed to be whipping in, making sure no one got left behind. Malcolm watched them all pass.

He stopped to cover his biodegradable pollution with scraps of grass and heather, and set off at a run to catch up. He had run some way along the path with no sign of anyone, when he came to the place where several paths crossed. He just caught sight of Tom Bolt's back disappearing round the hillside on the third path to the left.

It was then that he realized. He pictured the party strung out along the path, processing past him as he found relief, and he was sure. Jeffrey wasn't there. He couldn't have missed him, not in that outfit. His hat towered half a head over everyone else.

Malcolm yelled, 'Hey, Tom, stop,' but the hillsides only echoed his cry. The mist had turned to a soft insistent rain, seeping through clothes, moorland and even the rocks. A few sheep munched, unperturbed. Malcolm considered his options.

'I could catch them up and tell them Jeffrey's lost. But by the time I do, he will have come to the crossroads and gone the wrong way. I could just wait, or I could go back and find him.'

Malcolm thought for a moment or two. Jeffrey was the biggest nerd who ever wore Marks and Sparks Y-fronts, but he was his cousin. Malcolm went back.

He didn't have to go very far. Jeffrey was sitting on a rock back up the path and singing a plaintive chorus.

'I am not afraid, no, no, no; I am not dismayed, not me . . .' He even managed a jaunty wave of the arm, but his voice sounded reedy and nervous in the lowering greyness. One leg stuck out before him, a gap between the green lycra and the red socks uncovering an obviously swollen ankle.

'Malcolm! Hallelujah, the Lord sent you.'

'No, he didn't,' said Malcolm crabbily. 'It was the baked beans. Where the heck have you been?'

'Well, praise the Lord, it's rather wonderful really,' said Jeffrey, rubbing his ankle. 'The Lord gave me a mighty chance to witness.'

'And a mighty chance to get lost,' said Malcolm. 'Come on, we'd better get going before we lose them altogether.'

Jeffrey struggled to his feet.

'What d'you do to your leg?'

'Well, I was coming to that. There was this group of Germans and I stopped to give them a leaflet each. "Das ist le chemin, la verité et la vie," I said. Good, eh? Means "This is the way, the truth and the life". I learnt it on the Euro-outreach conference last year. They didn't seem to quite grasp it actually, but they took the tracts in the end. And then I saw this chap. He wasn't on our path, but another one quite a way off. And the Lord said, "This man is searching for a way," so I went to tell him.'

'And was he? Had he got lost?'

'No, I mean, he knew where he was in the heather and that, said he lived round these parts. It was metaphorical, don't you see? He was spiritually lost . . .'

Aren't we all? thought Malcolm.

'He was a pleasant chap. Quite odd—strangely dressed . . .'

You're saying that about him? thought Malcolm.

79

'. . . sort of hippie, punk type. Said he'd come here to find the meaning of life. Come to find himself. I put him right of course, told him he needed to find Jesus. We had a nice chat and he took a Gospel in the end. But he went off saying there were many ways up the mountain.'

'Yeah, well, there are, and many ways down again. If we don't get a move on, we'll be well and truly lost. What did you do to your leg?'

'Well, I thought of a verse to give him: Matthew 7, that's about Jesus being the rock, you know, so I went after him but I must have caught my foot on a stone.' Jeffrey's normally pasty face was even whiter with pain.

'Let me look,' said Malcolm. He touched it and Jeffrey winced. 'I bet you've sprained it. I did that in football once. You're supposed to bind it up.' He took his Danchester scarf and wrapped it tightly round Jeffrey's leg. Then he took off Grandad's braces and wound the elastic around the outside, tying it in a knot.

'Try that. Lean on me and take it steady.'

Taking it steadily, with a great deal of groaning on Jeffrey's part, and a fair amount of unspoken cursing on Malcolm's, they followed the path to the cross-roads. Once there they paused. It was clear that Jeffrey's ankle was not going to hold out for long.

Malcolm pondered. Yesterday had been bad enough. If he went off the path today Big Fin would chew him up and spit him out. What choice was there anyway? They had no map and no idea where they were. Surely, sooner or later, someone would notice they were missing and stop to wait.

'Come on, Jeffers,' said Malcolm wearily, 'It's only pain.' That was what Dad always said. 'Positive mental attitude, Jeffrey. I think we're going to have to give it a try.'

Slowly, with only grunts and groans breaking the

silence, they crept up the steep path to the ridge. There was no sign of anyone ahead of them. Eventually, after what felt like for ever they were poised at the top with the long ridge ahead of them. The path went right along the top, the rocks falling away steeply either side.

'Woh, hairy or wot?' said Malcolm.

They set off slowly, encased in the mist. They were about half way along when the mist lifted.

'Woh, what a view,' said Malcolm. Suddenly they could see it, distant peaks, the blue loch and the rolling moorland far below them. And just as suddenly they could see the sheer drop either side of them.

'Woh, seriously hairy!' said Malcolm.

A sort of groaning, gulping noise came from behind him. Malcolm turned. Jeffrey's face was as green as his hat.

'I er, I er . . . Can we just stop a moment?'

'Leg bad, is it?' asked Malcolm.

'Yes, I er . . .'

'Yeah well, it's only pain.'

'No, no, it's . . .'

'Look, we'll take it slowly. I'll go in front—too narrow side by side.'

Jeffrey groaned. He took a few steps, stood quivering for a moment, then sat down. 'I can't,' he said finally. 'I'm, I'm, I'm scared.'

Whatever happened to trusting the Lord? thought Malcolm. But he didn't say it. In a funny sort of way Jeffrey was being quite brave to admit he was scared.

'Yeah, it is a bit scary,' agreed Malcolm gently. 'The trick is just to look at the path ahead. Don't look down either side.'

Jeffrey struggled up again. He stared ahead, eyes wide and wild, but his legs refused to move. He sank down again.

'I can't,' he whispered.

Malcolm sat down too, wondering desperately what to do. Jeffrey closed his eyes and screwed up his face. *Praying,* thought Malcolm. *Fat help, that is.*

There they sat on the wet, cold, slippery rock, the whole of Scotland spread out either side of them, and unable to go forward or back.

'Look,' said Malcolm after a while. 'What if we crawl?'

I don't need to do this, thought Malcolm. *This is just for Jeffrey.* Nevertheless, the memory of yesterday's narrow escape made even the indignity of crawling seem like a good idea. And Jeffrey needed the encouragement.

'Look, I'll go first. All you need to do is keep your eyes on my bum and follow me.'

Jeffrey shook his head wildly.

'Jeffrey, don't be so pigging stupid,' said Malcolm firmly. 'We can't stay here all night, and I know you can do it. Come on, or I'll leave you there on your own.'

He knew he wouldn't, much as he'd like to, but the threat worked. He crawled forward, steadily and slowly and he could hear the groaning and scraping behind him as Jeffrey followed.

They were going steady, when a snuffling noise in front of him made Malcolm look up. A dog was bounding towards him and they met nose to nose. Behind the dog, strolling casually, an old weather-beaten man. A gun was crooked in his arm.

'Good day to ye, lads,' he called, as if meeting people crawling along was an everyday occurrence.

He skipped lightly down to a narrow ledge to let them pass.

'Excuse us crawling,' said Malcolm embarassed, 'but my cousin's hurt his leg.'

'Aye, ye're not the first ones to crawl the ridge,' said

the old man calmly. It was an excuse he'd heard before. 'But ye're a bit young to be up here alone.'

'We've got separated from our party.' explained Malcolm. 'You haven't seen them have you? There's about fifty—from the Adventure Centre.'

'Oh aye, young Findlay's crew. Passed them half an hour back.'

Half an hour! Malcolm groaned.

Jeffrey hadn't heard. He was delving in his puffball pockets for a leaflet.

Without looking up, he held out his hand. 'I wonder, sir, if you've found the path to eternal life? Can I offer you this copy of Mark's Gospel?'

The old man, whose clothes were as mottled and weather-worn as the landscape, looked at Jeffrey with puzzlement and some distain. 'I hae me own paths, mon.'

'Ah yes,' said Jeffrey, 'but the Bible says, "broad is the way that leads to destruction".' In his enthusiasm he looked up. He saw the drop and quivered noticeably.

'I ken what the Good Book says, lad. What I think on it's my affair.'

'Yes, but . . .'

Malcolm had to admire Jeffrey—even when he was green with panic he never gave up. But enough was enough.

'Jeffrey, shut up,' he said firmly. 'We're lost, not him. Please, sir, I think we need some help.'

The old man couldn't have been kinder once he'd understood. 'Ye'll never catch them up,' he said, 'and ye'd be daft to try. I'll show ye a good path down. Follow me.'

And with that he turned and was striding back the way he came. Malcolm stood up. 'Come on, Jeffrey. We're going to have to walk.'

And Jeffrey walked. Overcoming his fear he took the narrow way that led to safety. And it seemed only a few steps before they were in a dip on a wider path and the old man was issuing instructions.

'Ye say your buses are by the Loch. Well, this path will bring ye down to the car park in no time at all. Follow the path down to Grey Stone Valley. When ye come to the stream—the second stream, mind ye, not the piddling little one ye can step o'er—ye follow the stream to the left and take the path alongside it, the one that goes round the foot of Old Harry's Seat. When the stream goes off to the right, ye cut left through Fingle's Forest. Keep on that track and ye'll be in the car park. It's easy. I'll go back across to the ridge and tell young Findlay I've found ye.'

They found the path easily, just as the old man had said. Grey Stone Valley, Old Harry's Seat, Fingle's Forest...

Old Harry's Seat. Where had he heard that name before...?

Malcolm repeated the names to himself but there was no need. They were in the car park before they knew it. They were sitting there waiting when the others came round the loch. 'My baby has gone down the plughole' they sang as they marched.

Big Fin gave barely a nod to Malcolm and Jeffrey as they climbed aboard the minibus and the singing died away.

'Look here,' complained Jeffrey, 'you're in charge. I think you ought to examine my injury. I think I might need to go to hospital.'

Big Fin looked as if he could cheerfully dump Jeffrey in the nearest casualty unit, or even the nearest loch, but he patiently examined the leg.

'Unorthodox first aid,' he said grimly. 'Should have taken your boot off right away.'

He pulled the boot off with as much care as he could, but Jeffrey still writhed in pain.

'Will I be permanently damaged?' Jeffrey's face was as green as his ski-suit.

Big Fin made Jeffrey move the ankle around. 'Bit of a sprain. No problem. Rest it tomorrow.'

Jeffrey didn't look too upset about that. Tomorrow was watersports.

'And tomorrow,' Big Fin turned to Malcolm, 'you and I have some unfinished business. By the Land Rover, straight after breakfast. Getting lost once on my camps is *looking* for trouble. Twice is *getting* it.'

That evening the speaker told a Bible story. *Even I know this*, thought Malcolm as he sat dozing in the back row. *RE, Scout parades, they're always doing this one*.

He summed it up vaguely in his mind. *Mugger beats up bloke on lonely road. Holy Joes go by—too busy to stop. Next guy—some sort of ethnic minority, a type they don't like—stops and does the business. Bandages the bloke up, takes him to a hotel, pays the bill, then on his bike and he's gone.* Malcolm was glad God approved of practical stuff like that. *Better than all that singing*.

Jeffrey, his ankle stuck out prominently on a chair, shifted uncomfortably as the talk went on.

Must be hurting, thought Malcolm. *Perhaps I was a bit unsympathetic*. He yawned and closed his eyes.

Uh, uh, what? Malcolm jumped as the guitar struck up the last song. Jeffrey was staring at him again. Malcolm snapped his eyes shut again. *I'll punch him, I swear I'll punch him if he goes on at me again*.

At last the guitar's final twang died away. The meeting was over. Malcolm stretched and yawned and wondered if he could sneak off to watch telly. A shuffling noise made him turn to see Jeffrey hobbling towards him. There was a determined look in his eye.

Oh no, thought Malcolm. 'Must go, Jeffrey. Leg's looking better.'

Jeffrey sat down heavily and stuck out his leg between Malcolm and the door. 'Malcolm, the Lord's been showing me . . .'

I'll hit him, I will. Malcolm clenched his teeth and his fists. 'Not now, Jeffrey. I really don't think . . .'

Jeffrey was muttering something. '. . . swine,' it ended in a loud squeak.

'What?'

'The other day I called you a swine, spiritually speaking that is . . .'

'Yeah, well, you religious lot make me feel like a load of streaky rashers . . . spiritually speaking.'

'No, no, I was wrong. I'd still be on the mountain if it weren't for you. You turned out to be the Good Samaritan.'

8

BIG FIN'S RESCUE

'Right, we've got a job to do,' said Big Fin when Malcolm reported to him after breakfast. 'Getting that bike back.'

Malcolm sat in the front seat of the Land Rover feeling sorry for himself as they bumped up the narrow track. He felt sure Big Fin was just doing this as a pointless punishment. And he was missing windsurfing—the thing he'd most wanted to do in the whole week. They'd never get the bike back. Big Fin hadn't seen it, stuck there half-way up a sheer rock face.

'I went back to find it Tuesday evening,' said Big Fin. 'Wheels are badly buckled. Needs some repair, but it's worth salvaging.'

'But . . .' Malcolm was baffled. 'How?'

'Abseil down, like we tried Monday.'

'Oh, and then you'll be able to reach it?'

'Not me—you.'

Malcolm digested this information for a bit. Hanging off a little ten-metre face with grass underneath you was one thing. This was hundreds of metres and jagged rocks below.

'Wouldn't it be safer if you did it?' he ventured after a while. 'You've had such a lot more experience.'

'Didn't think you were that fussed about safety,' said Big Fin.

87

He pulled the Land Rover to a squealing halt. Word-lessly he went to the back and pulled out several coils of rope, a harness, a helmet, and a selection of metal clips and clamps. He gave two coils to Malcolm and set off up the path. Malcolm followed.

'I've met plenty of wallies in my time,' said Big Fin suddenly as they plodded up the path, 'wouldn't have thought you were one of them. What made you do it?'

Malcolm grunted. 'Dunno.'

'Funny, you seem quite bright to me.'

'Someone got up my nose.'

'So you wanted to prove something?'

'S'pose so.'

'What d'he do, this bogey-man?'

Malcolm looked at Big Fin. Matted beard, dirty corduroys, weather-beaten sinewy arms. *Why should he understand?*

'Must have done something.'

'Took the mick,' said Malcolm.

'So you can't handle a wind-up?'

'No . . . I mean, yes, I can. Usually. But he got to me. They did this thing about ambitions, and he saw my am-bition and he laughed.'

'Oh, right,' said Big Fin. He was silent for a while. 'Did that to me when I was your age. Thirteen, right?'

Big Fin—tall and broad as a Gladiator—had he ever been teased?

'How?' asked Malcolm. 'I mean, why?'

'Where I come from, my bit of Glasgow, being tough meant smashing bottles through windows or writing rude words on walls. If you were a real hard man, you nicked cars. If you weren't they got you. I wasn't quite as big then. And I wasn't like them, not after . . .'

They were there now, at the point where the path turned. Big Fin stopped and began sorting ropes.

'After what?' asked Malcolm.

'Once, just once, an old priest loaded some of us yobs in a rusty Morris Minor and took us to the mountains. And it was like "This is it!" I'd seen a TV programme about mountains and thought it was heaven. When I found out I could get there, that was it. I'd always hated school, but I came back and studied. Had a reason, see, a dream. I was going to get out. Didn't like that, my mates. S'pose they thought they'd never get out. So they took the . . . You got dreams then, Malcolm?'

'Yeah . . .' The word rose at the end, an unspoken *Why should I tell you?* And then it came, rushing out. 'I want to be a fashion designer, see, and this boy Colin made out I was a poofter. Said my clothes were rubbish. I think he's a nerd.'

'Colin Bell?'

'Yeah.'

'Hmmm,' said Big Fin. 'Trampled your dreams, eh? Don't let them, Malcolm, don't let them do it.'

'Well, I didn't want to. That's why I tried to beat him.'

'You nearly went, you know. You let a wally like Colin Bell drive you over a cliff. By rights you should be a stiff in a box by now.'

Malcolm bent and picked up the broken branch. Then he leaned over and peered into the quarry. The bike still hung, defying the odds, on the one bush in the entire cliff. Malcolm looked at the rocks far beneath. He shuddered and drew back.

'Don't worry,' said Big Fin, uncoiling a rope. 'It's safe.'

'I can't . . . I mean, how do I . . .?' Malcolm's stomach was suddenly full of a million colliding butterflies.

'Abseil down. You were fine on Monday.'

That was Monday, thought Malcolm. *Before all this.*

The crumpled bike suddenly made the dangers seem terribly real.

'Take another rope down with you,' continued Fin. 'When you get to the bike, attach the other rope to it with this...' he showed Malcolm a large metal loop, '... karabiner. Then I'll haul it up, and you climb up alongside.'

You climb up... Sounded easy when you said it quickly. Malcolm lay down on the outcrop of rock. His jelly legs were less of a problem that way. He forced himself to look over again. You couldn't even see all the rock face. An overhang obscured at least half from view. The bits Malcolm could see looked smooth as polished glass.

'Stand up,' said Big Fin. 'Harness.'

Malcolm climbed into the body harness. He stood still while Fin checked every fastening and clipped the rope to the harness. It seemed to take a long time. He tried to control the butterflies and concentrate, while Fin explained to him carefully about descenders, karabiners and prusik loops.

'It's perfectly safe,' said Fin. 'If you do what you're told, that is.'

He tied the other end of the rope around a tree trunk. It was a huge tree, and Fin leaned all his weight against the rope to check it. Still Malcolm pictured it uprooted and hurtling down the cliff after him.

'Helmet,' said Fin. Malcolm put on the helmet. It felt worryingly light.

'But... But... You said I'd have to climb up. I don't see...'

'These things,' said Fin, attaching some more metal loops to the harness. These had hand grips and sharp teeth. 'Jumars.'

'Oh, right,' said Malcolm.

'One for your hand and one for your feet. The minute you put your weight on them, the teeth grip the rope and hold you firm. Take your weight off one and move it up, then move the next one, and so on.'

Couldn't you just pull me up? wondered Malcolm, but he knew the answer. In Big Fin's eyes this was a test, a chance to prove himself.

'You pull yourself up, as I pull the bike up. Come up alongside, so you can free it if it gets stuck. Easy.'

'Er, yeah,' said Malcolm.

'Right,' said Big Fin. 'Over you go.'

Being suspended high over sharp rocks has a strange way of concentrating the mind. For the first time Malcolm felt truly sorry. He expressed it as 'I've been a wally,' but it was repentance as deep as any Bible-basher's.

However, being suspended high over sharp rocks gives you no time to dwell on things. Malcolm was lowering himself, slacking off the rope to let it through the descender, feet pushing gently off the rocks as he'd been taught. Gradually he got nearer to the bike. As he descended his stomach still felt scared, but his head knew he was safe. Big Fin, who had every reason to be angry with him, was in charge here, and Big Fin could be trusted.

He was level with the bike now, buckled, bashed and balanced precariously in the bush. The aim was to rescue it, but one false move could send it spiralling down to the rocks. Gingerly Malcolm edged towards it. For a moment the bike swayed, almost dislodged from its shaky nest—and then Malcolm had it, grasping the handlebars and slipping the karabiner round the frame as Big Fin had told him.

'Good,' called Big Fin. 'Well done. Now make sure

the bike's secure and free of the bush . . . Great. Now attach the jumars to the rope . . . Try them like I told you. Now remember, you're attached by the harness. Even if you let go, you won't fall. When I say, start to climb.'

It seemed impossible and it took for ever. The words of Fin's brief instructions echoed in his head. *Test it out. Take it slowly.* There was no danger of Malcolm doing anything else. He was far too scared. He stared resolutely at the rockface. Nothing existed except this slab of granite and these slender ropes. No way was he going to look down.

Once or twice he nearly gave up. 'My arms have had it,' he would call up plaintively to Big Fin. Or, 'I can't move my foot.'

'You've got the strength,' Big Fin would answer calmly. Or 'Yes, you can, just go gently.'

Malcolm was beginning to think he might make it, when—he was stuck. He had almost made it to the top, he was just under the overhang. Over on the right, the bike was hanging free, Fin kept on hauling and the bike disappeared over the top.

'Fin, what about me? Fin!'

There was no answer.

'Fin . . . Fin . . .' It was impossible. Malcolm couldn't get to the rope above the overhang. He tried to lean out, but tipped backwards alarmingly, so far that the deep grey pool and its surrounding rocks came into view.

Oh no—he was tipping, he was slipping . . .

No. The rope was holding.

'This is no time for acrobatics,' said an unflappable voice above him. 'Remember what I told you.'

Malcolm remembered and pulled himself upright. He felt his heart thumping.

'Now, push yourself round to the left. Good, good.' And Fin was guiding the rope, pulling it up.

After forty-five minutes that were forty-five hours, Malcolm was hauling himself over the top. His hands were stiff with cramp, his leg muscles ached. His stomach—hey, how weird, his stomach felt OK. He'd been so busy concentrating, he'd stopped feeling scared. Then he looked back at the way he'd come, and the butterflies danced once more. He lay flat on the rocky path and stared at the grey sky.

'Not bad,' said Big Fin casually.

Not bad—it was flippin' heroic, thought Malcolm, but he knew a 'not bad' from Big Fin was high praise indeed.

'You've got the makings of a mountaineer,' continued Big Fin, 'but shift yourself. It's coming on to rain.'

On the way home, as the Land Rover bumped over the moorland and sheep scattered in its path, Malcolm put words to the question that had been churning in his brain.

'D'you think the bike can be repaired?'

'Maybe.'

'How maybe? I mean . . . What I mean is, will it cost a lot of money?'

'What you mean is, will you have to pay?' said Big Fin, staring ahead through the rain-spattered windscreen.

'Well, yeah. I read the notice by your office. It says . . .'

'Guests are liable for damage caused by negligence.'

' . . . and I asked what it meant and they said it meant I had to pay.'

'You reckon you were negligent then?'

'I dunno,' said Malcolm. 'I know I was bloomin' stupid.' There was a long pause. 'Sorry.'

'D'you know if you're insured?'

'Shouldn't think so,' said Malcolm, thinking of the nicked TV and video. 'But how much will it be?'

'Well, a repair might be £100. A new bike is £350.'

'You see, well, I could get a paper round or something, but it would take a while. Dad's out of work, see, and he'll go totally spare if you tell him, and he won't have the money in any case.'

'Bit of a problem then,' said Big Fin, lighting up a cigarette. 'Looks as if we'll have to claim for it.'

'You mean your insurance will pay?' asked Malcolm, relieved. 'Oh, great. I mean, that's all right then.'

'Not exactly,' said Big Fin. 'The Centre's running at a loss. The more we claim, the more they'll charge us next year. Won't take much to tip the balance.'

'Oh.' Malcolm was silent.

'It'll sort itself out,' said Big Fin calmly. 'Things usually do.'

Raindrops tapped and bounced a rhythm on the windows. Big Fin breathed a gentle spiral of smoke.

'Things tough at home then?' he asked after a while.

The brackish smoke drifted across Malcolm's eyes. They were pricking with tears.

'Yeah,' he said.

'What sort of tough?' asked Big Fin.

And out it came, all the rows and tellings-off, how Dad ignored him and Mum nagged, how he felt so— useless.

'How d'you think your dad feels?' asked Big Fin.

'Well . . . useless, I suppose,' said Malcolm. 'But I don't see why. He's good at lots of things—engineering and carpentry and making models and playing football—and he used to be good fun.'

'Losing a job does funny things to people,' said Big Fin. 'If you do a thing long enough, you see yourself as what you do. You're not just Fred or Joe or Marlene, you're Fred the carpenter, Joe the footballer, Marlene the engineer. So if the thing gets taken away, it's like you lose yourself.'

Malcolm thought about it.

'I've never heard of an engineer called Marlene,' he said after a pause.

'Doesn't mean to say there couldn't be one.'

'D'you think being a fashion designer's a girly thing to do?' Malcolm was putting himself on the line here.

Big Fin stubbed out his cigarette in the overflowing ashtray. 'No.'

'You don't think it's cissy?'

'Not if it's what you want to do. Not if you do it well.'

The Land Rover rattled over the cattle grid and into the Adventure Centre. 'Hang on to your dreams, Malcolm,' said Big Fin as he swung out of the cab. 'Now, you can take that bike to the shed for me.'

The others were full of sailing and windsurfing, but Malcolm didn't mind. He could have boasted of his cliff-hanging exploits, but he knew better.

It was the final evening. Tomorrow they would all be scattered. Tough cities and leafy suburbs would swallow them up. Addresses were being exchanged. Promises to meet, to write. But it would never be the same. Friends they'd laughed with, talked late into the night with, would soon be just memories. Next week the same old routine would seem strange. The week after it would be normal.

It was time for the final meeting. There was a buzz in the air. This was when things were meant to 'happen'. What things, Malcolm wasn't sure. They sang the same songs, but louder. They did silly action songs that got faster and faster, till even Malcolm joined in and laughed.

And then the talk. The laughter died down. There was a deep hush. There was a special speaker tonight, good-looking, sincere as a TV presenter. His words poured out in a persuasive stream. Malcolm let them flow over him. Occasionally something made sense. Now and then ideas he would have liked to grasp floated past in a floodtide of jargon.

The words gushed and tumbled and at last abated. The guitarist began to play softly. *Uh huh*, thought Malcolm.

'Jesus is calling you now. It's time to repent,' said the smooth, sincere speaker. 'I want you to come up out of your seat and stand at the front if you know God is calling you.'

A few boys stood up and shuffled forwards. The speaker's intense blue eyes seemed fixed on Malcolm. 'There are more here. I know God wants to touch more lives. It may be you've never owned him before, well, now is the time.'

Malcolm shuffled uncomfortably in his seat. He looked round. Other eyes were looking at him. Jeffrey was in his 'head-bowed-in-hands' position.

If he peeks at me, I'll kick him, thought Malcolm.

'Don't delay,' said the tanned, bright-smiled preacher. 'God wants you now.'

Malcolm found himself rising to his feet. As if under compulsion he pushed along the row. He moved slowly forward, nearer and nearer. He was coming to the front, and he was there—the door marked Exit. Two more steps and he was out.

A watery sun had just dipped behind the flat-topped mountain. Somewhere far off a sheep bleated. Smoke rose from the meeting-room cabin. The smell of burning logs mingled with the scent of fresh pine.

Blindly Malcolm stumbled over the needly floor of

the forest. He felt hot and angry and he didn't know why. He made his way to the stream and climbed down to the rough wall that channelled its flow. He sat huddled on the chilly stone, staring at the rushing water.

Why does everyone want me to change? This lot want me to repent and be all happy clappy. Jeffrey wants me to be a Jesus freak like him. Dad wants me to be an engineer like him, Grandad wants me to play for Danchester, 'cos he never did, Mum wants me to be neat and tidy and never play loud music. I'm not even good enough for God, apparently. No one likes me as I am.

He threw sticks into the tumbling water and watched them race away.

Razza likes me. And Marty and Si and Jamie. Least I think they do. P'raps it's just that we enjoy the same things. Do they really care about me—me inside—or do we just hang out together? Does anybody like me just 'cos I'm me? He couldn't answer that question.

The mountains were getting darker. Up above a thin crescent moon and one bright star appeared.

Is anyone really out there? thought Malcolm. He stared at the one twinkling star. As he did, others appeared, more and more, dotting the sky with mystery. Another smell joined the wood smoke and pine needles. It was Golden Virginia, and a red glow approaching showed that Big Fin was coming out for his evening hand-rolled cigarette. In one hand he held a beer bottle and he hummed a tune to himself as he scrunched over the pine carpet.

He stood for a while, eyes raised to the distant peaks. After a few moments he spotted Malcolm. He strolled over and dropped onto the wall.

'Not into meetings, eh?'

Malcolm grunted.

'Me neither.'

'It's all this religious stuff,' grumbled Malcolm. 'They keep telling me Jesus wants me to repent or sing songs or be a sunbeam or something. If God made me Malcolm Crouch, why's he so keen to turn me into something else?'

'Who says he is?' asked Big Fin, swigging from his beer bottle.

'They do. I mean, you're normal. You're not a card-carrying Jesus freak like this lot.'

'How d'you know?'

'What?'

'How d'you know I'm not a card-carrying Jesus freak?'

'Well, you don't go to meetings and sing and wave your arms around or give out leaflets or thump a Bible around.'

'Doesn't mean I've never read it.'

'Oh.'

'Not easy, is it, sorting out what's God's stuff and what's the stuff other people put on you?'

'No . . . How d'you know?'

'Read a bit, think a bit, swill it round in my head. Sort of chat with the Almighty—when I'm walking round, like. After a while you sort of know.'

'Oh.' Malcolm chucked a stone into a deep brown rock pool. 'You see, I've never said this to anyone before, but I've always thought, if there was someone out there, I'd like to know him . . . or her, or it. But I suppose I thought whoever it was wouldn't want to know me.'

'Knows you already,' said Big Fin. 'Course he knows what he made.'

'Doesn't mean he likes me.'

Big Fin picked up a pine cone and twirled it in his fingers as he tried to string his words together. 'Seems to me, if God had wanted to make us all the same, he could've. Would've made life a lot easier, I'd have thought. Must've taken a lot of effort to make everyone of us different. Fingerprints, faces, everything. All in a little bit of DNA. Clever. If he went to all that trouble, I reckon he likes you as you are.'

'So I don't need to change?'

'Didn't say that.'

'But I don't like singing. And I'd laugh in the wrong places.'

'That's OK. That stuff's optional.'

'You mean you don't have to sing choruses with a silly grin?'

'Nope, or chant psalms with a po-face. Can if you want to, but they're not part of the package.'

'Well, what is?'

Big Fin screwed up his eyes in concentration. 'Love—not the sloppy sort, don't mean that. Treating people like people, saying thank you, saying sorry, listening. Letting God make you more like him . . . and more like you. Same thing really.'

They sat side by side in a long deep silence. An owl hooted. A bat swooped silently, barely visible, jet black on inky blue.

'Well, better go,' said Big Fin. 'See you, Malc.'

'See you,' said Malcolm. 'And thank you.'

He sat on the bank staring at the darkness. Then he began to move. He took off his shoes and socks and lowered himself into the rushing stream. The coldness made him gasp. He bent down and cupped his hands in the tumbling water. He lifted his hands and dashed the water over his face. The icy droplets exploded like stars in the darkness.

'OK, God,' he whispered, 'Help me be me.'

Then feeling slightly foolish he scrambled back to his shoes and socks.

Lights were going on in the dormitory cabins. Chatter wafted over as the others came out of the meeting. There was a mega-midnight feast stored under a floorboard in Cedar Cabin, and a raid of retribution planned on Oak Cabin. They had it coming after the stink bombs. Malcolm smiled to himself as he went back to join the others.

9

PASSING SHIPS

It's one thing to believe in God in the mountains. It's something else again when you get back home.

If there was a Devil—and Malcolm wasn't even going to begin to figure that one out—he'd have felt right at home at 27 Lavinia Close.

The semi-detached from hell, thought Malcolm as he looked gloomily around him. It was the week after his return and he was eating spaghetti from the tin. Stacey was on the phone rowing with Matt. They'd split up, she told Malcolm. For a couple who'd split up, they spent an awful lot of time rowing.

Mum was in the kitchen crying over a stack of papers. Malcolm had seen them. There were several bills printed in red with ominous warnings 'if this amount is not paid within . . .', and one from the bank that said 'Dear Sir or Madam, at the close of account yesterday your account was £750 overdrawn. Please take steps to remedy this situation.'

The steps Mum was taking involved working 8a.m. to 6p.m. at the supermarket, six days a week. The money still wouldn't go round. She was exhausted, weepy, and now she'd gone on strike.

'Get your own food. I'm sick of the lot of you,' she'd announced one day when she came in to find three hungry faces looking hopefully at her. 'Malcolm, you can do your own smelly washing for a change.'

Dad was upstairs in bed. He wasn't ill, he'd just taken to lying there all day, letting a grey stubble cover his chin. He emerged now and then to fill his tarred mug and leave another tea-bag on the draining board. Mum had stopped cleaning too.

Dad emerged now, scratching his belly under his vest and wiping an accusing finger over the dust on the sideboard. Malcolm sensed a storm brewing and slipped up to his room.

God, this is terrible, thought Malcolm as he lay on his bed and stared at the cracks in the ceiling. *Well, do something,* came back a voice in his head. *Who me? You must be joking. What could I do?* The voice was silent. He lay gloomily listening to the rise and fall of argument downstairs. He put on his Walkman to block out the noise and stared aimlessly at the splodges on the ceiling where he'd once thrown his Super Slime. A fly buzzed round the room. Malcolm's eye followed it to the top shelf. It landed on a dusty Airfix model of a galleon—never quite completed.

He stared at it for a while. After a few minutes he got up. He stood on his bed to reach down the model and blow off the dust. 'I must be daft,' he muttered to himself. 'Still, anything's worth a try.'

He burrowed under his bed for a box of paints, delved in a drawer for brushes, knife and a tube of glue. He piled them all together with the galleon and went downstairs.

Dad was slumped on the sofa. Hiccupy sobs came from Mum in the kitchen. Wordlessly Malcolm got an old newspaper and spread it on the table. On it he stood the galleon and laid out the remaining spars, bowsprits and nautical accessories. He'd lost the instructions, of course, but he still had the picture on the box. Carefully he began to glue bits on.

Dad pretended not to notice, and Malcolm pretended concentration.

After a while Dad looked up. Malcolm was still gluing, really concentrating now, the tip of his tongue poking out of the corner of his mouth.

It was that tip of a tongue that did it. It was a little boy's tongue. A little boy with freckles and grubby knees, not yet too big to ask Dad for help. It was the tip of a huge iceberg of memories, and Dad sighed as visions of happier days came flooding back.

Malcolm would have died, of course, if he had known he was doing it. But he didn't, and it worked. Dad shifted in his chair, noticed his stained vest and remembered when he'd had a clean white shirt every day.

Malcolm was beginning to get bored by the time Dad stood up and came over. 'That doesn't go there. It's a cross-piece, not an upright.'

'How d'you know?' retorted Malcolm, automatically a teenager again.

Dad showed exaggerated patience. 'Because it's slightly wider. Look, all the cross-pieces are thicker.'

'Yes, but . . .'

Dad stepped back. 'Pardon me, I was only trying to help.'

'Oh, yes, well, um, you could be right, I s'pose.'

Dad sat down at the table. 'Yes, I see your point. What if it goes there . . . ? No . . . Are you sure you haven't got all these bits wrong?'

'Oh, Dad, come on. They all fit.'

'Yes, but they'd fit on the other mast as well.'

'Well, maybe, but I haven't got the instructions.'

'Yes, look, they do. You can see on the picture where they all go wider.'

'Hmm, well, they're there now. I'm not taking them all off again.'

'Oh come on, if a thing's worth doing . . .'

' . . . it's worth doing well.' Malcolm muttered the old refrain. 'Yes, but Dad, it's only for fun.'

'Never mind. That's how you learn. If you can't get things right in your hobbies, you'll never get them right for real work.'

'Well, I'm still not taking them off now.'

'Oh, don't be so ridiculous.'

'It's not ridiculous. I think they look OK.'

'But it's not right.'

'It's only a model.'

'Only, only . . . Nothing matters to you, does it?'

Malcolm and Dad glared at each other. Malcolm opened his mouth. The words had already formed in his head. *You can talk. Look at yourself. What matters to you these days?*

But he shut his mouth, stared wildly at Dad a moment longer, got up and left.

The retort wasn't needed. Dad's own words hung in the air, echoing back at him. As Malcolm slammed the front door behind him, Dad put his head on the table and wept.

Malcolm's eyes were glistening too as he walked fast and aimlessly down the street. *So much for that idea. Keep your head down, Malcolm. Leave well alone. You'll only make things worse.*

He saw Razza coming towards him, kicking a can. Razza was a good mate, but Malcolm couldn't face his mates right now. Razza hadn't noticed him, but he would soon. Malcolm turned the corner. Razza did too. Malcolm saw a familiar bungalow, half-hidden behind trailing honeysuckle. He swerved left and hid behind the trellis, while Razza kicked his unobservant way past.

Malcolm stood under the arch, heavy with scented flowers, and rubbed his eyes. He remembered his other idea. Oh well, he was here now. He rang the bell.

'So what I thought was,' explained Malcolm as he sipped Mrs Walenski's hot, sweet tea, 'if I made a whole batch of waistcoats—with my pocket money I could get material for about six—and then sold them at the school boot fair, then I'd have enough money to save some and make another six, and so on. It wouldn't take that long, and then I'd have enough money to get us a new telly.'

Mrs Walenski beamed her approval.

'Only I'd have to do it here, 'cos Dad thinks sewing's cissy and he'd only moan.'

Mrs Walenski nodded. 'You do . . . I help . . . But . . .' she struggled to express herself. 'Way . . . waysi . . . waistcoat,' (a triumphant smile) 'still here.' She pointed to the shelves.

Malcolm remembered. He'd been trying to forget. Helena's waistcoat. He went to the shelf and picked it up. Almost finished, only a few stitches here and there to add the final touches. He'd left them deliberately. If he finished it he'd have to give it to her, and if he gave it to her she might not like it, and if she didn't like it . . . He thought about Robbie Greenall . . . He didn't want the risk.

But he couldn't explain that to Mrs Walenski. He could hardly explain it to himself. He replaced the waistcoat on the shelf.

'Yes, but what about these other waistcoats? I was hoping you'd help me work out how much material I'd need.'

Mrs Walenski drew her pad of paper towards her. She could still do sums, it seemed. It was only the words that got lost between her brain and her voice. Inside she was bright as a button, a head full of frustrated enthusiasms. She could even figure the difference between yards and metres. She gave him both, written on the back of an old shopping list.

'Thanks,' said Malcolm and stood up. She looked accusingly at Helena's waistcoat. 'Oh, OK.'

He sat down and added the final stitches. It looked good, though he said it himself.

Mrs Walenski stroked it lovingly with her distorted hands. 'Ex-cel-lent,' she said, giving each syllable a deliberate weight. 'Your girl like this. Your girl lucky.'

But she's not my girl, thought Malcolm, as he made his way home. *Nor ever likely to be.*

As he came into the living-room, Dad started up from the table. Malcolm noticed a few more pieces had been glued on the galleon. He noticed something else. Two crisply ironed white shirts hung over a chair.

'Has Mum come off her strike then?' asked Malcolm.

'No . . . er, no,' said Dad staring almost guiltily out of the window.

Dad? Dad ironing shirts? 'Oh, right,' said Malcolm and made his way upstairs.

There was a note tacked to his bedroom door. 'Marty called. Phone him back.'

Malcolm hadn't seen a lot of Marty recently. He'd finally got lucky with Sonya Harding and went round these days like a man under orders. *Women do terrible things to your mates,* reflected Malcolm as he tapped out the phone number, *perhaps they're a bad idea.*

'Malc!' Marty's gruff half-broken voice sounded urgent. 'Do you still fancy Helena?'

Did he? Malcolm's heart was pounding at the very name.

'She's all right,' he said casually. 'Why?'

'Well Sonya says she was talking to Helena at the video shop and Helena thinks you're quite nice but she thinks you don't like her.'

'What about Robbie Greenall?'

'Robbie? Oh yeah, that sixth-former creep. Yeah, Sonya says they all fancy him and Helena was really gone on him for a while. He asked her out a few times but it was only to watch him doing his disco and it got boring. And then it was all groping in the back of the van and his breath smelt of garlic.'

Buy some breath freshener. Malcolm made a mental note. 'So, why you phoning?'

'I just thought you'd want to know,' said Marty aggrieved. 'Me and Sonya thought.'

'Yeah, but I mean, it's holidays now. I'm not going to see her for weeks.'

'Yeah but . . . me and Sonya thought . . . We're going to the pictures tomorrow night. Why don't you ask Helena and we'll all go?'

Why not indeed? 'But how can I ask her if I don't see her?'

'Easy, phone her up. Sonya's got the number.'

'Oh er, I don't know. I mean, I don't know her that well. I mean, suppose I get her mother. I know, you ask her.'

'Me? I can't ask her.'

'Well, Sonya then.'

Sonya could be heard giggling at the other end of the phone.

'OK, Sonya says she'll ask.'

'So . . . When? How? When will I know?'

'Oh, we'll phone you up when it's fixed. No rush, is there?'

'No . . . No.'

'I mean, it's not as if you're madly in love.'

All the next day Malcolm paced anxiously. The phone's gentle bleating made him twitch and jump. It was always for Stacey or Mum. Dad wore a thundercloud on his brow and told Malcolm he was a restless layabout. Malcolm retreated to his room to play Leadbitter Riff and twitch in private.

By mid-afternoon he had given up. *If they'd fixed it, they'd've phoned by now. I'm going out.*

Passing downstairs he noticed Dad was working at the Airfix galleon again.

Malcolm caught a bus to town and went to Peggy's Fabrics. He made sure no one from school was around before he went in. He'd never been in that sort of shop before. Well, blokes didn't, did they?

Huge rolls of material were stacked in every available space. At the front were soppy floral cottons, the sort that dinner ladies wore under their overalls. Behind them were pyjama stripes, tough denims and oddly, army camouflage. Malcolm thought about making a combat jacket. Behind that were the evening fabrics. It was hard to imagine there was much call for them in Danchester, but here they were: nets and chiffons, gold sequin, silver lamé, black and silver stripes. Malcolm thought about a rock singer's jacket, stars and stripes in silver and black. He ran a hand along the fabrics, lost in a world of possibilities.

An officious cough made Malcolm turn to face a round lady in spotted crimplene and stiff-permed hair. She eyed Malcolm suspiciously. 'Can I help you?' She looked as if she doubted it.

Malcolm produced his sheet of measurements. 'Yes please, I want some material for waistcoats.'

Once she had made sure he wasn't going to stick chewing gum on her best velvet, or shoplift scissors for some heinous crime, Peggy was quite helpful.

Malcolm staggered out of the shop with silk for backing, brocade for fronts, buttons, threads and some machine needles thrown in.

Mrs Walenski's name had proved a magic 'open sesame' to the world of dressmaking. 'Ah my dear, what a woman,' said Peggy with a sigh. 'Such a shame. Those hands—a tragedy. The flower of a generation; we won't see her like again.'

Malcolm took his fabrics back to Mrs Walenski's and started cutting out. He tried not to think about phone calls.

When he got home, Dad was painting the galleon. His face was skewed in concentration, his tongue pushed into his cheek as he peered at his meticulous work.

'Hey, that's good, Dad. Brilliant,' said Malcolm.

'If you're not going to bother, I thought I might as well,' Dad said testily. All the same, he almost smiled.

Malcolm went to raid the kitchen.

'Oh, by the way, someone phoned. Michael, Mark?'

'Marty?'

'Yes, probably. He said it's on for tonight, meet them in the burger bar.'

'McDonalds?'

'Mmm, probably. 7.30 in town.'

Malcolm left the kitchen. What did food matter at a time like this? Shower, clean teeth. *Why didn't I buy that breath freshener?* Squeeze a few zits, iron a shirt. Waistcoats—wear the waistcoat, yes, why not? Take hers? No, not today. Play it cool this time. He hoped there'd be a next time.

His heart started to thump. 6.45 already, no time to lose.

He was early. McDonalds was still full of kids. Noisy kids having a party and whingeing kids with weary over-shopped parents who needed more than a Happy Meal to cheer them up.

Malcolm slid into a window seat, stared at the High Street and pondered his problem—cash flow. He'd spent all his money on the waistcoat material. He might just manage one cinema ticket. He hoped Marty could lend him the price of a coke.

Malcolm smiled anxiously at the girl who came to clear his bare table. 'Waiting for someone,' he explained.

'Enjoy your meal,' said the girl absently. As long as they paid her to wear a silly cap and wipe tables, she couldn't care less what the customers did. Malcolm didn't know that: he just felt guilty.

7.30 and his heart began to pound. No one came. Well, Marty was late everywhere. Even Sonya couldn't work miracles.

7.50 and the girl in the red cap, a philosophy student from Senegal, was sweeping round his seat. 'Still waiting,' said Malcolm apologetically.

7.55. In the Burger Star in Bridge Street Marty, Sonya and Helena were finishing their milk shakes. 'He's always late,' said Marty. 'Hark who's talking,' said Sonya. Helena stared out of the window and fiddled with her earrings.

8.05. Malcolm's heart was sinking. It was all a joke. They'd set him up to look an idiot. The philosophy student approached again with the table spray. It was time to go.

8.10. 'Look, we're going to be late for the film,' said Sonya. 'Perhaps he didn't get the message,' said Helena hopefully. 'Nah, I told his Dad, he said he'd write it down. He might have something else on.' 'Let's just wait a little longer,' said Helena.

8.12. *Perhaps I got it wrong,* thought Malcolm. *But Dad did say McDonalds. No, I said McDonalds! He said yes. He said burger bar. Burger bar? Burger Star!* Malcolm was racing up the pavement to Bridge Street. The rubbish sacks were out on the pavement. Outside the florists were some tired and tattered flowers. Among them Malcolm spotted a rose, almost perfect. He paused to grab it as he ran.

8.14. 'Come on,' said Sonya crossly. 'It's Hugh Grant. I don't want to miss the beginning.' Helena looked up and down the empty street before they turned the corner to the cinema.

8.15. Malcolm came panting round the corner and into Bridge Street. He slammed into Burger Star. The Turkish brothers who owned it looked up, bored.

Malcolm stood wheezing. 'You wish to order?' asked Hassan politely. Malcolm looked blank for a moment. 'Er, no, was there a girl in here? Good looker, long hair. With a boy my age and another girl.'

Hassan spread his hands in incomprehension. The cafe was full of long-haired girls and boys his age. Ahmed, slicing kebab, came to the rescue. 'Just left. Boy, two girls.' He pointed up the road.

Malcolm was running frantically. There was a crowd outside the cinema. Yes, that was them, Marty's blond stepped hair, Sonya's long frizz and a glimpse of reddish brown that must be Helena. As he got to the cinema they were disappearing into the door marked Screen 2. Malcolm dashed for the door. 'Ticket,' said a youth impassively. Malcolm dashed to the ticket office. A queue of people glared.

'Oi, get to the end,' said a red-faced woman.

'My friends, they've gone in,' explained Malcolm.

'Wait yer turn like everyone else,' said a greasy man in an Iron Maiden T-shirt. He was a large man. Malcolm slunk to the back of the queue.

'One in Screen 2,' said Malcolm.

'Three-fifty,' said the girl mechanically.

Malcolm counted his money—£3.32.

'It's gone up,' he said accusingly. 'I didn't know.'

'Bin up six months now,' said the girl disinterestedly. 'Next.'

Malcolm kicked his way miserably back down Bridge Street. That was it, a chance gone for ever. She'd think he didn't care. Think he was scared. He stuck the rose in the bank's letterbox. So much for romance.

Then he saw it! 20p glinting silver on the pathway. He picked it up and dashed back to the cinema.

'Screen 2? Sorry, full up,' said the girl.

In a public phone box just outside Burger Star, Georgie Climes was dialling a number from a bit of paper. 'You know you told me to tell you if I saw that bloke in the waistcoat around again. Well, I just did. Can I have my tenner now?'

10

TRUE LOVE'S PATH

'So it all went wrong,' explained Malcolm as he sat in Mrs Walenski's pinning waistcoats. 'Nothing ever goes right for me.'

Mrs Walenski just nodded. She smiled her gentle lop-sided smile. 'The path... of true love,' she said, 'never... ran smooth.' It was a rare long sentence for her, dredged up from her memory.

'When you met Mr Walenski, I mean, was it, like, love at first sight?' Malcolm would never dare ask other grown-ups a question like that. They got all stiff and prickly. But somehow Mrs Walenski didn't seem to mind. She just smiled a sad sort of smile and struggled out of her chair. It was getting more of a struggle these days, Malcolm noticed. Once she was up she still managed her slow shuffle round the bungalow, but getting up was a major achievement.

'No, no, I do,' she insisted when Malcolm tried to help. 'Arms tired, that all. Arms not work good.'

Malcolm watched anxiously as she pushed herself up on her tired arms and struggled to her feet. There was a long shuffle-clunking pause as she made her way to another room. Malcolm wondered if he had offended her after all. She was in the little spare room, full of boxes and parcels. He could hear her there, laboriously moving things with her not-good arms and her long-handled pincers.

She returned eventually with a large box sticking from the basket which hung on her frame. In this basket, rather like those on an old-fashioned bicycles, she carried everything she needed—food, letters, newspapers, flowers—from A to B. It was just one of the things she'd got down to a fine art in managing to live. The home help came in the morning to do the cleaning and get everything ready for the rest of the day. Water in a kettle, milk in a thermos flask all ready on the table. Mrs Walenski couldn't carry hot drinks. Sandwiches cut and ready in the fridge. Mrs Walenski couldn't spread butter.

'You look,' she said, clicking the kettle on with her stick. She opened the box. It was full of letters, old and yellowing, tied in batches of blue ribbon. From among the letters she took out a faded brown photograph. A stiff young man in uniform gazed sternly out over the decades.

'Stefan,' said Mrs Walenski. 'Stefan Walenski.'

'He was a soldier, then,' said Malcolm.

Mrs Walenki nodded.

'Was he a soldier when you met him?'

'No, no.' She was scrabbling through the box, until she found what she sought, another photo. Same young man, moustached this time, cigarette in mouth, trilby hat jauntily on one side.

'I work . . .' Mrs Walenski mimed pushing a needle in and out.

'You worked at sewing?'

'Ah, sewing. Stefan on bike. Come each day.'

'He worked there too?' queried Malcolm.

'No, no, come on bike.'

'Deliveries?' tried Malcolm.

'Ah, deliveries,' repeated Mrs Walenski. 'School too, school at night, for lo . . . lo . . .'

'Law?' tried Malcolm.

'Ah, law. We marry.' Mrs Walenski found another picture, black and white this time, a tiny bright-eyed girl beaming at the camera. She wore a white lace dress and carried a huge bouquet. She held the arm of the man in uniform who looked proudly down at her.

'You looked pretty,' said Malcolm. 'And he looks nice.'

He put the dog-eared photo on the table. Mrs Walenski picked it up. She stared at it, lost in thought.

Malcolm was silent. A strange sadness hung in the room. He looked at the letters in their pale blue ink. They were all in a foreign language. Words of love poured out in a strange tongue.

'What happened to him . . .' he asked eventually, 'Mr Walenski?'

Mrs Walenski laid down the photo. 'Killed,' she said, 'in camp.'

'Oh.' Malcolm didn't have words for such things. 'Sorry.'

Mrs Walenski was pushing up her sleeve. A row of numbers were tattooed on her arm. 'Camp,' she repeated.

Malcolm stared blankly at the numbers. He remembered films, TV programmes, history projects.

'Concentration camp?' he asked.

Mrs Walenski nodded. She pointed to herself. 'Jewish,' she said.

She was quietly and calmly making the tea. Malcolm busied himself with his pinning. His mind carried pictures from those films and projects: skeletal figures in strange striped pyjamas, piles of bones, heaps of old shoes, smoking chimneys, blank-eyed survivors.

He tried to apply these images to the bright-eyed girl and the jaunty soldier. Tried to apply them to a wrinkled old lady in Broad Heath, calmly offering him a cup of tea.

'But,' he said eventually, 'you're always cheerful.'

'I am alive,' she said simply. 'Living is good. I have worked. Work is good.' She waved her arms around her. 'I have home. To live under... under my own vine—that is good.'

Malcolm followed her gaze to the pendulous purple flowers round the French windows. The creeper was invading, he noticed, pushing its curling tendrils through the cracks in the window.

The garden! He had a sudden pang of guilt, noticing the knee-high grass.

'I'll cut your lawn tomorrow,' he promised.

'Ah, you good boy.' Mrs Walenski beamed, but she rapped his knuckles with her stick. 'Now, waistcoats,' she said.

It was on Saturday after mowing the grass that Malcolm found out about the chair. Mrs Walenski had a leaflet—a special chair that lifted you up when you wanted to stand.

'That's a great idea,' said Malcolm. 'Are you going to get one?'

Mrs Walenski just smiled and shook her head. She pointed to the price printed very small in a corner of the leaflet—£1,000.

'Gosh, really, just for a chair with a motor. That's stupid.' He thought for a moment. 'Listen, I bet my Dad could make you a chair like that. He's an engineer. He can make anything.'

Mrs Walenski's eyes brightened.

'I'll ask him. Have to choose the right moment. He's out of work, see. He's got plenty of time. Dunno what he'll say, but I'll give it a try.'

The Airfix galleon stood on the dining table. Its plastic

flags fluttered stiffly in a non-existent breeze. Tudor roses adorned its prow. Tiny cannons gleamed black and gold. Dad was feeling better.

Alongside the galleon was a pile of wood off-cuts. Dad had decided plastic was too easy. He was going to carve the next galleon.

Mum came out of the kitchen with a plate of tuna macaroni.

'Clear this table, then,' she demanded, but her voice was warm. 'You can get your own. They're in the kitchen.'

Dad's ironing had provoked a truce. Mum cooked again now, but she wouldn't wait tables or wash up. She washed clothes but didn't iron. It wasn't quite peace in the Crouch household, but there was definitely an absence of hostilities.

Malcolm decided to float his suggestion. 'Dad.'

'Mmm.'

'There's this old lady round the corner. She's got arthritis and she's had a stroke.'

'Mmmm.' Dad was reading *Naval warfare in Tudor times*.

'Well, she can't get out of her chair and it costs a thousand quid for a chair that lifts her up, and I thought: Dad could make something like that. My Dad could design one half the price.'

Dad put down his library book. 'I suppose I could, yes. I could work out a design, no problem.' Flattery works on parents like anyone else.

'So could you make her one?'

Dad looked at Malcolm, and Malcolm watched the self-esteem drain from his face.

'Oh, yes, no problem. I mean, I've got a fully-equipped workshop in the back garden, haven't I? I mean, it's only a few grand for lathes and milling tools and upholsterer's wages. Easy, no problem. Course I can do it.'

117

'Oh.' Malcolm pushed macaroni around his plate. 'Oh, never mind. It was only a thought.'

'And since when have you been hob-nobbing with old ladies?'

'Oh, er, oh. They sent us from school. Community studies. I went to cut her grass.'

'Hmmm, glad they do something useful at that school of yours. Where's she live, this old lady?'

'Just round the corner—Gladstone Drive. You know, that bungalow on the corner.'

'Hmmm, cutting grass. Thats about all I'm fit for these days. At least that's what people seem to think.' He glowered at Mum. 'Fat chance I've got of ever being an engineer again. Even for bloomin' old ladies' chairs.'

Dad banged his fist on the table. He caught the edge of a plate and tuna macaroni erupted all over the table. A bit caught on Dad's glasses, hanging there as he scowled angrily. Silliness on top of shock made Malcolm laugh. Mum laughed too, pointing helplessly at the macaroni eyebrows. Dad swore violently and stormed out, slamming the door behind him. Mum's laughter turned to tears and she bolted to the kitchen.

Malcolm sat alone at the spattered table. *Another fine mess*, he told himself.

The summer holidays dragged on. Everyone else was away. Marty had gone to Bulgaria, Sonya was at Butlins. Malcolm's hopes of Helena seemed dead and gone. She was probably on a beach somewhere too. The only thing Malcolm could do was make waistcoats.

It was a Friday in late August and the first batch of waistcoats was nearly finished. Five hung almost complete from the picture rail, adorning Mrs Walenski's walls while Malcolm put the finishing touches to the sixth.

And that wasn't all. Mrs Walenski had insisted on paying him for cutting the grass. With the money he had bought more fabric, and the next batch of six lay on the table, patterns pinned on and ready to cut. There was snooker on the telly (Mrs Walenski's favourite), mugs of tea and a packet of jaffa cakes. All was peaceful when the doorbell rang. Malcolm got up.

'No, you work,' said Mrs Walenski, struggling up. 'I go.'

She shuffled out taking her purse for the milkman. The milkman liked to tell Mrs Walenski about his allotment and the progress of his onions. A different voice today though. *Relief milkman*, thought Malcolm. *Everyone's on holiday*. It was a familiar voice, though, and it wasn't talking about milk.

'I gathered you needed a new chair,' said the voice. 'I've been thinking and I may have come up with an idea that could help. My son . . .'

Dad! Malcolm froze. He heard Mrs Walenski's puzzled groping for words and Dad's explanation. At last she must have been satisfied. Malcolm heard the door swing wide and the shuffle-clunk along the corridor.

Malcolm leapt from the chair, sweeping up pattern pieces from the table and waistcoats on hangers from the wall. He dumped them behind the old sofa. Frantically he twisted the knob on the French window. It turned halfway with a grinding sound. The voices came nearer. All Malcolm could think was that Dad mustn't find him here. How could he explain? The knob turned with a rusty squeal. Malcolm slipped out into the garden.

Mrs Walenski's voice carried out to him as she came before Dad into the room. 'Ah, Malcolm, good boy, sewing, working, here now . . .'

Malcolm pulled frantic faces from behind the glass. He caught her eye and shook his head wildly.

119

'Ah, not sewing,' said Mrs Walenski. 'Grass. I have had a stroke. Words bad.'

Malcolm dashed to the coal house and got out the mower. Up and down the grass he went like a creature possessed. He'd cut it yesterday, but who was to know?

'Malcolm good boy,' Mrs Walenski was saying. 'Good boy.'

'Er, yes,' said Dad in amazement. 'But why is he cutting the grass in the rain?'

Malcolm's secret was safe. Mrs Walenski had played along—one occasion where lack of words came in handy.

Dad had gone away and thought about the chair. The table was littered with drawings, but in the end he'd had to admit defeat. 'I'm afraid I really can't do anything without a proper workshop,' he told Mrs Walenski a week later. 'But I have had a few other ideas.'

This was what Dad was good at. He watched, he thought, he found solutions.

'Your light switch. Look, if I put in an extension lead you can have the switch next to your chair. And your tea. Why don't we put it on a trolley next to your chair? And look, I've made this little frame on rockers. Then you don't have to lift the kettle, you just tip it over on the rockers to pour.'

And Mrs Walenski beamed and Dad went back and pottered happily with wood and metal in the garden shed, and Malcolm carried on his secret life of making waistcoats.

No one suspected the waistcoats, but they did suspect Malcolm.

'Where are you going?' Mum would ask.

'Out,' Malcolm replied.

'But where?'

'Out, just out.'

And the door would bang behind him with Mum saying, 'I'm worried about that boy. I never know what he's up to these days.'

Dad would nod. 'No hobbies, no interests, it's unhealthy.'

'And those boys he goes round with. They're not nice lads, I'm sure they're not. I saw that Simon Parker smoking the other day. On drugs too, I shouldn't wonder.'

But right now there were no boys for Malcolm to hang out with and he was bored. He took to walking over to Helena's end of town, just to see if he could catch a glimpse of her.

He was there one hot, dusty end-of-summer day, outside the newsagents sucking an ice pop—a pathetically small 10p ice pop like the little kids have, it was all he could afford. He was sitting on a bench and wondering idly where he'd seen those two men in the old Cortina before. One was black, one white, and they seemed to be staring at him.

He played a game of staring back, contorting his face and rolling his eyes. *Don't mess with me,* he told them inwardly. *I'm a psychopathic loony.* He slumped sideways, went boss-eyed and scratched under his arms to make the point.

'Oh, hello,' said a voice.

Malcolm's whole body did a spine-tingling, heart-stopping lurch as Helena slipped onto the bench beside him. He straightened up, man-of-the-world, and slipped the ignoble ice pop down to his side.

'Is this yours?' asked Helena. 'Can I have a lick?'

There were harps playing as Malcolm made his way down Disraeli Drive. There were bluebirds fluttering over the tortilla factory, rainbows over the rec. Fireworks exploded around him in glorious fizzing bursts as he strolled—no, skipped—home.

He had a date. A date! A date with Helena who didn't seem to think he was a psychopathic loony or a zitty kid. He had to admit she didn't think he was a debonair man-about-town either; she wasn't fooled that easily. But he was a person, a person who was OK to hang out with. Perhaps even a friend. They talked about music, school, euthanasia and earrings. She even laughed at one of his jokes. And they had a date!

7.30 tomorrow evening outside the cinema. There was only one cinema. He'd earn a fiver cutting Mrs Walenski's grass tomorrow. This time nothing could go wrong.

7.15 on a glorious, golden evening, and Malcolm was setting off for town. He was wearing his waistcoat and a shirt he'd ironed carefully three times. He'd borrowed Stacey's hair mousse, Dad's aftershave and the mouthwash Mum got when she had a gum infection. Malcolm couldn't afford breath freshener, so this was the next best thing. It tasted like something you'd clean lavatories with, so he reckoned it must be working. Anyway, they never had garlic in the Crouch household. Mum would think it was something you planted and grew spring flowers from.

In his hand, Malcolm clutched a carrier bag. Not just any carrier bag—an ancient and faded Harrods bag that Mrs Walenski provided—and in it wrapped in tissue was the waistcoat. The precious waistcoat he'd made for Helena. 'To everything there is a season, A time for every purpose . . .' and now was the time—the time to give Helena his cherished, laboured-over gift.

How would she take it? Would she giggle, scorn it, get embarrassed? Would she give him a smile, maybe even a kiss? Would she think he was a cissy? It was make or break time, but he had a gentle fluttering gut-stirring hope that this time he might just make it.

He played cloud spotting as he crossed the foot-bridge. One purply-blue cloud looked like a cat—Garfield perhaps—another one was definitely a Biker Mouse from Mars. Another pink cloud looked like a reclining woman, a reclining woman with big . . . Malcolm blushed a little and tried to think of something else. That one's a steam engine with a . . . AAAAAAARGH!!

Malcolm lay on the footbridge in a pool of blood. His Oxfam waistcoat had been torn from his body and ripped apart. Only a few silk threads remained. The Harrods bag lay empty and crumpled by his side. The purple tissue drifted across the bridge in the gentle evening breeze. In the distance two men raced to a car. There was the sound of an engine, then silence. For a moment Malcolm's hand twitched. He tried to lift his head. It hurt—a huge, heavy pounding ache. He tried to think, to remember what had happened. He called out, a feeble strangulated groan, but there was no one there to hear. He lowered his head again and everything went black.

Above him the clouds made a kaleidoscope of colour and shape. Gradually they darkened and merged with the night.

Outside the cinema, Helena paced, first patient, then angry, then hurt. As she set off for home she hardly noticed the sirens racing through the town.

11

HOSPITAL VISITS

The first thing Malcolm saw was the policeman. *There's a cop in my bedroom,* he thought hazily. The light dazzled him and he turned his face into the pillow. It was throbbing—not the pillow, his head. It smelt odd—no, not his head, the pillow. It was stiff and white and cool, not his usual well-worn, friendly Bart Simpson. It was all very strange but thinking was far too difficult.

Malcolm drifted back into oblivion.

When he woke again, the policeman had gone. In his place sat Mum and Dad. The white dazzle had gone now, only a dim light that seemed strangely far away. He woke again in the grey dawn to find Dad still there, his head nodding and jerking in sleep. As Malcolm stirred, Dad jerked upright. He leant over and grasped Malcolm's hand. He looked frightened. Malcolm was surprised to see tears in his eyes.

He didn't get it. Had Mum and Dad had another row? Why had they given him these stiff itchy sheets? He ached a lot. He was so tired. So tired . . . It was all too muddling. He didn't underst . . .

'I don't understand,' said Mum. 'Why should anyone do it?'

'Drugs. We think it might be drugs-related, Mrs Crouch.'

Cathy Crouch sat stunned. A policewoman put a gentle arm round her and offered her another cup of tea. 'That's why it's important we search through Malcolm's things. It might give us some clues.'

'But Malcolm, why Malcolm?'

'There's been a spate of gang-warfare in Danchester recently, Mrs Crouch. Mostly on the Donwain Estate across town, but it's been spreading. And it's all drugs-related. Kids on speed, dealers trying to get local kids to push for them. Then there's competition. They're all fighting for control of the same patch.'

'But Malcolm, not Malcolm.' Mrs Crouch twisted and turned a damp tissue in her hands.

'Two strangers have been seen in the area recently. Older men, not locals. They were spotted last night. We have reason to believe they may have been meeting your son.'

'He's only thirteen, for goodness sake.'

'It happens, I'm afraid. Can you tell us his movements recently? Do you always know where he is?'

'Well, no, not always. He's out quite a lot.'

'Do you know where he goes?'

'No, he doesn't tell us.'

'Has he been secretive?'

'Well, yes, a bit.'

'More so recently?'

'Well, yes.'

'Who does he go out with?'

'I don't know really. He hasn't brought any friends home for a while.'

'Have you noticed any change in his personality? Is he moody or difficult, incommunicative?'

'Well, yes. He's a teenager, isn't he?'

'More so recently?'

'Well, yes, but . . .' Mrs Crouch screwed the tissue to a tight ball in her fist. 'You see, things haven't been very good at home recently and . . .' She tailed off, her chin quivering.

'It's often a trigger, I'm afraid,' said the sergeant wearily. 'Now, Mrs Crouch, if we could just search your son's room.'

Mrs Crouch dabbed her eyes with the paper ball. The policewoman automatically handed her another tissue and the ball joined the others in a soggy shredded pile on the table.

In the hospital, Malcolm lay still, a small figure in a white bed. He was guarded on each side by silent sentinels.

On one side a drip hung over him, steadily replacing his body's lost fluids. Beside it on a small machine a green line blipped regularly and reassuringly.

On Malcolm's other side, Dad kept watch, wakeful now and staring at his son as if seeing him for the first time. Around him the ward busied itself into life, but he remained motionless.

The hours passed and the hospital routine ebbed and flowed, but the still-life tableau remained the same. Occasionally Mr Crouch closed his eyes. Bob Crouch was not a praying man, but he was praying now.

At a service station on the M1 a blue Cortina pulled in. Two men, one black, one white, were arguing. Once more they pulled apart the two waistcoats. They sifted through torn threads and linings.

'Nothin, piggin' nothin,' said Scarface.

'You was the one who was so convinced this was it,' said Scowler, scowling even more today.

126

'She told me,' said Scarface. ' "Find the waistcoat," she said, "I think that's it".'

'Well, it wasn't,' Scowler snarled as he ripped the vivid silks and satins to a pile of rags in his rage. 'Neither of them . . . Why's there two anyway?'

''ow the 'eck should I know?' muttered Scarface. 'All I know is our chance of a few grand's gone—all in shreds.'

'Why do people think crime's easy?' complained Scowler. 'They ought to do this job.'

Scarface picked up the shredded waistcoats and dumped them in a rubbish bin. They lay there unseen, a vivid rainbow of rags and threads, as coke cans and cigarette packets were tossed on top. Later that day the bin men took them to a landfill site near Milton Keynes.

Helena was buying a Mars bar when the headline caught her eye.

'Provincial drugs war erupts—teenager left half-dead.' It was one of those school photos they always find when there's a murder or an accident. Cheerful face, tufty hair, looks like . . . looks like . . . oh no! Horror-struck, Helena read the details. 'He seemed so nice too,' she murmured to herself.

'You gonna buy that?' asked Mr Patel, but Helena wasn't listening.

Men and women in white coats came and stood over Malcolm. They shone lights in his eyes, stuck things to his head, pressed things on his chest, pushed needles into his arm. He was vaguely aware of events around him now, though none of it made sense. He saw Mum sometimes, or Stacey, they always looked solemn. And Dad, Dad was always there, grey and anxious with stubble growing longer on his chin. When the pain was bad, or the throbbing got worse, he found Dad holding his hand or stroking his head. Malcolm tried to smile or say thank you, but nothing seemed to be working right now.

It was always easier to close his eyes and go back to sleep, though sleep was never restful. Strange colours tumbled through his dreams; faces: white eyes in a black face, black hands covered with blood and gold threads, a man with hair like a haystack, the glint of a knife. There were clouds in his dreams, sunlit, racing, always forming into shapes, but he could never quite make out what they were.

And then one day the clouds cleared. He opened his eyes and saw a light fitting, a perfectly normal light fitting in a dirty cream ceiling. A face swung into view, a kind Asian face above a blue tunic. She smiled at him and he smiled back.

'Hello, Malcolm,' she said.

'Er, hi.' Malcolm was surprised to hear his own voice. The face disappeared.

'Mr Crouch, Mr Crouch, come quick.' The voice was going away. Other faces came round the bed, the white coats again, more blue tunics, and then Dad, his hair in messy tufts and his face creased in a huge smile.

And then there was Mum, crying and laughing, and Stacey saying he could borrow her hair mousse and she'd never be cross again.

And then it was the turn of the men in bomber jackets, patiently asking questions. It started coming back, the footbridge, the crack as his head hit the concrete, someone—more than one—behind him pulling at his waistcoat. The knife, glinting as he struggled, ripping into the waistcoat, plunging into him.

Questions, questions, questions, over and over again till Malcolm longed once more for sleep.

'No, I don't know who they were . . . Yes, I have seen them before . . . I dunno, just around . . . Well, different places, the school disco, the shops, I dunno.

'Why . . . I dunno why . . . Not much, only a fiver . . . Drugs? Course not . . . Honest, I dunno . . . Just hanging out usually, with my mates . . . No! My mates aren't into drugs . . . Why should I tell you who they are? . . . Going to the pictures . . . I told you, I've never taken anything, I'm not that stupid . . .

'No! I didn't know the men.

'No! I've never done drugs.

'No! I'm not in a gang.

'No! I don't know why!'

And then it was Dad's turn, shaved now, his brow furrowed with doubt.

'Malcolm, you've got to tell them all you know.'

'I have, honest.'

'But it doesn't make sense.'

'It was just a mugging. I don't know why.'

'People say they've seen you with the men before.'

'Rubbish.'

'Well, where have you been going? You've been out evening after evening.'

'Just hanging out, with my mates.'

'Your friends say they haven't seen you.'

'They were on holiday, that's all.'

'So where were you?'

'Out.'

'Where?'

'Just out.'

'Doing what?'

'What's it matter? It wasn't exactly much fun at home, was it? Moans and nags, Malcolm, do this, Malcolm, you haven't done this right. Not even a bloomin' telly.'

'You've been worrying your mother sick, you know. Don't think we haven't noticed your behaviour—sullenness, rudeness.'

'But I haven't done anything.'

'Look, son, tell the truth, no one will mind.'

'Not mind, you must be joking. I've never done anything right as far as you're concerned.'

'Look, I want to trust you.'

'But you don't, do you? You never have.'

Malcolm turned his head away and burrowed into the cold unfriendly sheets. Dad swore in frustration and got up. Malcolm heard his footsteps going away down the ward.

There followed more interrogations, more rows.

Malcolm ached in places he didn't know he had and his head still throbbed. At night his dreams were full of wild confusions that left him worn out by morning. On the rare occasions when he slipped into deep peaceful sleep, there was always some bright friendly nurse or an earnest junior doctor, choosing that exact moment to take his temperature, offer him pills or adjust the drip.

Malcolm felt lousy, and feeling lousy fuelled his anger. *Some maniacs jump on me out of the blue, and everyone thinks its my fault. Everyone's making out I'm a pill-popping dopehead, whose idea of a good night out is a knife fight in a dark alley. Why should I tell them what I do? Whatever I do's wrong. Whatever I say they don't believe me.*

So Malcolm sulked and Mum pleaded and Dad got grouchy and the police sent kind child psychologists and tough detectives by turns, and still nobody knew why Malcolm had been attacked on the footbridge.

One day Dad was there when a different detective came. Dad and Malcolm sat without speaking, watching athletics on the telly. The detective was young and nervous, in a trench coat two sizes too big.

'Ah, Malcolm,' he said trying to be jovial. 'Sorry to disturb you again, young man. Just a few more questions, I'm afraid.'

Malcolm grunted.

'These waistcoats,' said the detective. 'We wondered if there was any significance in them.'

'What waistcoats?' said Dad.

'Malcolm was wearing one, Mr Crouch, and carrying another, isn't that right, Malcolm?'

Another grunt.

'And the attackers took them. Now have you any idea why, Malcolm?'

'No,' Malcolm gritted his teeth. 'I don't know why. Perhaps they had waistcoat phobia. Perhaps they thought I was a poof. Perhaps . . .'

'Wait a minute,' said Dad. 'What were you doing with two waistcoats? I know you had one—that ghastly flashy thing—why two?'

'Just 'cos,' said Malcolm.

'Why?' asked Dad in a voice that thundered round the ward.

'It really would be quite helpful to know, Malcolm,' said the anxious detective.

'It was a present,' muttered Malcolm. 'A present for a girl. I had a date.'

'And where do you get money to buy girls waistcoats?' demanded Dad.

'I didn't,' said Malcolm in a very low voice. 'I made it.'

'I'm sorry?' said the detective, struggling to hear as the crowd on TV cheered the 1,000 metres.

'I made it,' shouted Malcolm defiantly.

Dad just looked at him, blank and uncomprehending.

'This is a hobby of yours then, is it?' asked the detective.

'It's no hobby I've ever seen,' said Dad.

'You made it at school?'

'No.'

'Malcolm, did you steal the waistcoat? Please tell us, we all want what's best for you.'

The detective fiddled with the collar of his outsized trench coat and tried to look kind and concerned.

Dad fiddled with his glasses and looked totally perplexed.

Malcolm fiddled with the sheets and looked at each of them in turn. At last he said, 'Look, I made the waistcoat at this old lady's house—Mrs Walenski.'

Dad looked up.

'That's where I've been when I've been out. Round at Mrs Walenski's making waistcoats.'

The detective drew out a notebook. 'What name was that? Address?'

As Malcolm told the detective about waistcoats—the one from the charity shop, the one for Helena, the new ones to sell—Dad sat in deep and ominous silence.

After the detective had gone, Dad merely said, 'Why didn't you tell us?' in a flat, noncommittal voice.

Malcolm's reply was just as flat. 'I didn't think you'd like it. You'd say I was a poof. You'd say it was girl's stuff.'

'Since when did you care what I liked?' asked Dad.

Malcolm didn't answer.

'What say have I got in what you do? Why should you care about my opinion? No one else does ... It's better than being a junkie,' he acknowledged grudgingly, 'or a gang member. But why the heck didn't you tell us?'

Malcolm stared blankly at the screen. 'Why the heck should I?'

Dad got up and slowly left the ward. On the TV gleaming and sinewy athletes were receiving medals. Malcolm sighed and closed his eyes.

12
DRONGO'S SECRET

While Malcolm dozed in hospital, Mum and Dad went round to see Mrs Walenski.

'Ach, poor boy,' she said, and got out the six nearly-finished waistcoats and the six nearly cut-out ones for their inspection. 'Good, yes?'

Dad went very quiet.

'So he was really round here a lot?' asked Mum.

'Ah yes, work, working much. Good boy. He make boo ... boo ...'

'Beautiful,' suggested Mum.

'He makes beautiful way ... way ...'

' ... waistcoats.'

'Ah, waistcoats. You proud.'

She turned to Dad as she said this, but Dad turned away.

'But what was he doing them for?' asked Mum.

Mrs Walenski pointed to the TV.

'Something to do with a programme?' guessed Mum.

Mrs Walenski shook her head. 'Sell them, buy TV,' she explained, 'for you all.'

Dad looked up. He reached out and fingered one of the almost completed waistcoats.

'Good, yes,' repeated Mrs Walenski.

'Yes,' said Dad, 'good.'

'I wonder where he thought he'd sell them,' said Mum.

Mrs Walenski scrabbled through her pile of papers. She drew one out that said 'Boot Fair, Broad Heath Comprehensive, Saturday 25th August, 8.30a.m.'

'What a shame,' said Mum. 'He won't be out of hospital by then.'

'You finish?' asked Mrs Walenski hopefully.

'Me?' Mum's voice raised to a squeak. 'I've never been any good at sewing. And I'm working six days a week as it is.'

Mrs Walenski turned to look at Dad. Dad pretended not to notice. 'You have time?' she persisted. 'No?'

'Yes, but ... It's not my sort of thing, I'm afraid. Definitely not, I'm an engineer.'

Mrs Walenski continued to look at him. Mum looked at him.

'I help,' said Mrs Walenski after a while. 'I teach.'

'It's not that,' said Dad. 'I'm sure you're a very good teacher. It's just that ... It's not my sort of thing, really, not my sort of thing.'

'You do it. You could. Not too difficult. I help.'

'No, well, I mean, obviously it's not too difficult. I mean, I'm used to working highly complex machines. I'm used to working to the most detailed specifications. I'm highly skilled. I'm ...'

Dad's blustering died away. He looked up to find Mrs Walenski's eyes on him, amused and quizzical.

'Ah,' said Mrs Walenski. 'I see. Too good ... too good for needle.'

'No, no. Obviously that's not what I mean. It's just that ...'

'He thinks it's women's work,' said Mum after a moment's silence.

'Pah!' was all Mrs Walenski had to say to that. She

began to pull the waistcoats towards her with her stick. Dad got up to leave.

'I'm sorry,' said Mum as she followed him out. 'We're very grateful, honestly.'

Later that evening there was a ring at Mrs Walenski's doorbell. Suspicious, she put the chain on the door and looked out. Mr Crouch stood there, sheepishly adjusting his glasses.

'Look, if it would help, I'll make the waistcoats. By machine, of course. You wouldn't expect me to do hand sewing.'

Mrs Walenski smiled and shook her head. 'Of course.'

'You see, a man in my position, a qualified engineer. And I'd rather no one knew about me doing it. They'd think I'd gone soft.'

'Of course,' said Mrs Walenski. 'You come tomorrow.'

So the next day, Dad cut pattern pieces and pinned them together, and even—at last, with a slightly pained expression, sewed a seam.

'Not bad,' said Mrs Walenski. 'Not bad for a be . . . be . . . beginner. Hold here, and here. Let it move. No push. Now, straighter this time.'

Dad squared his shoulders, glared at the sewing machine as if it were the enemy and pressed the foot pedal once more.

In hospital Malcolm wore a slightly pained expression and looked at his visitor as if he were the enemy.

The visitor was Cousin Jeffrey, sporting a 'Jesus is the real thing' T-shirt, purple jogging trousers, sandals and socks.

'Look, Malcolm,' he was saying, 'I believe the Lord has a hand in all this. You know, sometimes he brings us to crisis point to show us the need to repent. Your drugs problem could have gone unnoticed for years if...'

'I haven't got a drugs problem,' said Malcolm.

'Well, praise the Lord. You see. It's a fresh start. It's all behind you now.'

'I never did have,' said Malcolm.

'Look, you can tell me,' said Jeffrey, leaning forward, 'in confidence. As a Christian, I accept you no matter what—hate the sin, but love the sinner, that's my motto.' He lowered his voice and leant over conspiratorially. 'Did you know, Malcolm? God loves you no matter what you do. I guess you may find that hard to...'

'Yes,' said Malcolm, thinking of the mountains. 'I know that.'

'... though your sins be as scarlet ... I beg your pardon?'

'I said I know. God loves me as I am.'

'Oh, well yes, of course, I'm glad you've accepted that. But I feel I should share with you the need for repentance. Do you know, we had this ex-junkie from San Francisco last week. Amazing. His life was a testimony, God can free you from the most harmful addiction.'

Malcolm sat up in bed. He drew a breath and announced in a voice that carried into the Ward Sister's office, the waiting room and the brain of a man still anaesthetised after heart surgery: 'Jeffrey, I am not a junkie. I never have been. I'm not addicted to anything—not unless you count rock music or Twix bars. I'm OK! ... OK?'

The heart patient sat up and opened wild blank eyes. The ward sister came running.

'Sorry, nothing's the matter,' muttered Malcolm, embarrassed. 'I'm OK, honest.'

Dad's glasses had slipped down his nose. His tongue was in his cheek as he pushed the completed waistcoat outside in. He held it up and smiled triumphantly.

'I reckon that's OK,' he said.

'OK,' repeated Mrs Walenski. 'Not bad. Now try again.'

Not again, thought Malcolm, as a gaggle of white coats stood round his bed. They goggled and prodded and said 'Now Malcolm' this and 'Malcolm' that, until he thought seriously about biting the hand of the next doctor who held his jaw to look in his eyes.

He was glad he hadn't, however. The consultant stepped back, puffed out his chest as if it was his own personal miracle and proclaimed, 'Pulmonary puncture, ladies and gentlemen, consequent haemorrhaging—and ventilation required. An excellent recovery.' There was a breath of admiration. 'Now Malcolm, how would you like to go home?'

Malcolm grunted. *What do they expect me to say? No, I'd much rather stay here and listen to old men groan and eat terrible food and be bored out of my skull?* So he merely grunted, but he couldn't hold back a smile.

'WELCOME HOME MALCO' said the banner hung across 27 Lavinia Close.

'It would have said Malcolm, but I ran out of space,' explained Stacey, giving him an uncharacteristic hug.

Everyone was being so nice to him. Malcolm couldn't understand it. He had waited in vain for Dad's explosion about the sewing, but it hadn't come. He hadn't been called a cissy or a big girl's blouse or a nancy boy—in

137

fact, Dad had been quite nice whenever Malcolm had seen him in the last week or so. He hadn't been in the hospital that much, only saying mysteriously that he was busy.

Mum was OK too. She'd been given a week's compassionate leave from the supermarket. Her eyes were less red-rimmed, less grey-shadowed—in fact, there was even mascara and crinkly smiley lines around them today.

In the living-room the Airfix galleon still flew its plastic pennants, the wooden galleon stood half-carved beside it. But it was what he saw alongside them that made Malcolm gasp. His waistcoats, all twelve of them, neatly finished and ironed.

'Dad did them,' said Stacey, twisting her face in an unsubtle wink behind Dad's back.

Malcolm's mouth hung open.

Dad came in from the car with the black plastic sack of Malcolm's belongings. He looked a little abashed.

'Thanks, Dad,' said Malcolm solemnly. 'You shouldn't have.' Then his face slowly spread into a grin. 'After all, it's women's work really.'

If Malcolm thought that being back home meant life was back to normal, he was in for a surprise. For one thing, although the pain had gone, he still felt so ridiculously tired. He'd get up in the morning feeling normal, and one hour later he'd be back in bed again. But perhaps that was just as well, because then Inspector Helm, the man in the oversized raincoat, came to visit.

He drew some photos from his briefcase. 'Now, are these the men who attacked you?'

'I've seen them before. They were at the disco. They were staring at me outside the newsagents.'

'But did they attack you?'

'I don't know. I saw a black hand with the knife. And it was a white hand on my shoulder—I think. But I didn't see their faces.'

'We found two dyed yellow hairs by the spot. Other people have identified these men. Your neighbour Mrs Sedge says she's seen them hanging around here.'

'Good old Beryl, twitching the curtains again,' said Dad.

'But the point is,' continued the Inspector, 'even if we could find them, we couldn't arrest them. No positive identification—not for the attack. And still no motive. It's difficult to pursue if we don't know why. We've come to the conclusion it was a case of mistaken identity. We've put you in the clear. But even so—who were they after? And why?'

'And who are they?' said Malcolm. 'That's what I want to know.'

'We know that,' said the Inspector. 'They're Londoners, in the gang world, petty criminals, but vicious. Two armed robberies and a GBH between them. We know who. What we don't know is where. They've disappeared. No trace at all.'

He looked apologetic. 'So, Malcolm, it may have been pure accident that they got you, and we've no evidence that they're in the area, but we still think you ought to stay indoors for a few weeks. Just until we're sure. You can go out by car, with an adult, but don't walk round Danchester on your own... If only we knew what they were after.'

'A prisoner in my own home,' groaned Malcolm, staring at the crack in the ceiling. 'Boring, boring, boring. I'd settle for anything to break the monotony.'

There was a ring on the doorbell, followed by footsteps on the stairs. 'Jeffrey's here,' said Mum brightly, ushering him in.

'Well, almost anything,' muttered Malcolm to himself.

Jeffrey perched his spindly frame on the edge of the bed. 'Good to see you, Malcolm. Sorry I haven't been around for a while. Been on a course—"How to spread the faith"—found it quite challenging, you know.'

I hope you're not going to practise on me, thought Malcolm, but Jeffrey was delving in his pockets. 'I brought you a present.' He deposited a rectangular package on the bed. Malcolm opened it to find a cassette and two Twix bars. Jeffrey beamed enthusiastically. 'I know you like rock music. I'm told this is, er, grunge. It's a Christian band.'

Malcolm sighed. *Religious grunge—sad or what?* But the Twix bars were thoughtful. 'Thanks, Jeffrey.'

Jeffrey looked suddenly hesitant. 'I'm sorry I didn't believe you about the drugs—and, er, I like the waistcoats you made.' He paused again. 'Would you, that is, I wondered if, if you thought it was a good idea, would you make me a waistcoat? When you're better, of course. And if you think it'd suit me. I'm not very good about clothes,' he confided. 'Perhaps you could advise me.'

Malcolm's jaw lowered.

'You know, I've been thinking,' said Jeffrey, rushing on in what was clearly an effort, 'I think maybe I'm a little out of touch with modern youth culture. I wondered if you could help me. Introduce me to your music, give me the correct words. For instance, does one say "Right on" these days, or "Far out"? I feel I lack credibility somehow—or should I say street cred!' His face brightened. 'And in return, perhaps I can take you for a trip in Ebenezer.'

Malcolm's mouth was wide and his eyes were narrowed as Jeffrey bounded to the window. 'Look, she's all mine.'

Malcolm came to the window and followed his gaze. Outside was an elderly, dented yellow car—a Lada. There was a rainbow sticker on the front window, and a pair of fluffy dice hung above the dashboard. There was a sticker on the back window too. Malcolm couldn't read it but he could guess what it said: 'Honk if you love Jesus' perhaps, or maybe 'Don't follow me, follow Jesus'.

'The dice were already in it,' explained Jeffrey, 'but I thought they looked quite jolly. Isn't she a beauty?' He clasped his hands and sighed.

'Er, yeah, Jeffrey, terrific.'

'I've been saving for a while, you know. It's a bit of an extravagance, when you think of famine in Africa, so I didn't want to get anything too flashy.'

'Er, no, Jeffrey.'

'But she goes pretty well, only stalls now and again. Ebenezer means "Thus far hath the Lord helped us". Good name, isn't it? Incidentally, did you know that Moses rode a motor bike?'

'Er, no.'

'Yes, we know because the Bible says "the sound of his triumph was heard throughout the land." Ha, ha, ha, ha.'

A joke! Jeffrey's cracking a joke? Fortunately Jeffrey laughed enough for the two of them. Malcolm was gobsmacked.

'But about the music,' continued Jeffrey. 'Explain to me about the sort of music you like.'

So Malcolm played Genetic Prawn and Leadbitter Riff and showed Jeffrey his *Rock On* magazines and his Leadbitter Riff tour programme.

'Mmm,' said Jeffrey, trying very hard to find something to appreciate. 'It's lively, isn't it? Pity you can't hear the words.'

Jeffrey thumbed through the tour souvenir book as he listened. He paused at a picture of Drongo Leadbitter. 'D'you know, that looks just like the chap I met up in the mountains. You know, when I hurt my leg.' He examined the picture more closely. 'Hair a bit longer. Could swear that was him.' He flicked through the blurred performance photos, then stopped and peered. 'Doesn't that waistcoat look like the one you used to have?'

Malcolm peered too. The picture was fuzzy. Drongo strutting his stuff, distant on stage. It was fuzzy and yet familiar.

'Yes, it is. Just like it,' said Malcolm.

'Well, what a coincidence,' said Jeffrey. 'Now is this what you'd call heavy metal?'

But Malcolm wasn't listening. He was thinking about a Scottish mountain in the mist. He was remembering an old man saying 'Now take the path round Old Harry's Seat.' He was thinking about it because he'd suddenly remembered where he'd seen the name before. On the scrap of paper they'd found in the waistcoat pocket.

'This bloke you met up the mountain, does this look like him? And this? And this?'

Malcolm was flicking through the magazines. At each picture of Drongo, Jeffrey agreed, 'Quite similar', 'Remarkable', 'That's definitely the chap.'

'What did he say, Jeffrey, when you saw him?'

'He said he'd come to the mountains to find himself, he wanted a simpler lifestyle—I got the impression he lived not far away. I witnessed to him about the Lord, of course, and then I tripped, and then he went off.

Only a seed sown, but the Lord brings the harvest in his own ...'

'That's it,' yelled Malcolm. 'A simpler lifestyle! That was Drongo Leadbitter you saw. And the waistcoat—the waistcoat had the clue. Old Harry's Seat, Old Harry's Seat—now what else did it say?'

What had he done with the scrap of paper? He'd taken it out of the pocket, he remembered that. It was at Mrs Walenski's. It was gone. Thrown out long since. Whatever did it say? He searched his memory in vain. Mrs Walenski—she'd been there. She might remember.

Malcolm leapt up and grabbed Jeffrey's knobbly elbow. 'Jeffrey, how's about we go for just a little trip in Ebenezer?'

Jeffrey and Mrs Walenski both wore expressions of profound bafflement. Malcolm, so excited that he was hopping up and down, tried again.

'Mrs Walenski, when I brought my waistcoat here, the first one, it had a bit of paper in the pocket. It got thrown away, but I just thought you might remember what it said. Something about Old Harry's Seat.' He paused, with the air of someone trying very hard to believe in a miracle.

Mrs Walenski shook her head slowly, then stopped. She pulled toward her the pile of papers which always occupied one corner of her table.

'No, it was ages ago. It got thrown out. You wouldn't have it now.'

Mrs Walenski fished out a dog-eared piece of paper. On one side was written: 'Malcolm Crouch, 27 Lavinia Close,' and on the other:

> *Down beneath Old Harry's Seat*
> *Down behind Old Harry's feet*

Silent music where waters flow
Hidden where strangers never go

'That's it! That's it! "Silent Music"—that's what he called it.'

'Who called what?' asked Jeffrey blankly.

'Leadbitter Riff—that's what Drongo called their last album—the one that never got released. The one they hid away, where only someone with a simpler lifestyle— buying things in Oxfam—and a love of beauty—an embroidered waistcoat—would find it. That's it! And of course, of course, that's why!'

Jeffrey and Mrs Walenski exchanged worried glances.

'Look, Malcolm, you've been very ill,' said Jeffrey gently. 'You're probably trying to take things a bit too quickly.'

'But don't you see?'

'No, I don't see,' said Jeffrey firmly. 'Do you, Mrs Wa... Wa...?'

'Walenski,' said Mrs Walenski. 'I don't see.'

Malcolm drew a deep breath as if to explain something extremely obvious to very small children.

'Leadbitter Riff made their last album, right? Then Riff Pritchett overdosed and died. So Drongo decided to give it all up. He destroyed all the copies of the recording except the master, and he hid that one. He said whoever found it, it would be theirs. He said it would be someone with a simpler lifestyle and a love of beauty. And this is it! This is the clue!'

Malcolm waved the scrap of paper in excitement. Jeffrey and Mrs Walenski looked at him blankly.

'So,' said Jeffrey slowly, 'That's why you were attacked.'

'Yes, yes, that's why—the waistcoat. I don't know

how they knew. But if they thought it was the clue—that's even more proof.'

'Ah.' Mrs Walenski beamed. She had given up trying to understand what it was all about—was Drongo a dog? Was it a picture album?—but she could see Malcolm was happy and that was enough.

'But,' Jeffrey's mind was still ticking over. 'I know it's nice music—if you like that sort of thing—but I can't see why anyone would want to kill you for it.'

'No, no, it's not just the music. Although imagine—holding your very own Leadbitter Riff original in your hand.' Malcolm sighed. 'Course it's not just that. Who-ever finds it gets all the rights, all the sales profits. Can you imagine how much that would be? Millions!'

It was only as he said it that the full implications dawned on Malcolm. 'We could pay off our debts. Set Dad up in business. Get a telly, and a video. Get you a chair, Mrs Walenski.'

Mrs Walenski beamed even wider. Her eyes sparkled with delight. She thought about it again—a dog had buried a photo album under a seat... She took the paper from Malcolm and read it again. 'Beneath Old Harry's Seat?' Her voice rose at the end, to show it was a question.

'It's in Scotland,' explained Jeffrey. 'We've been there. It's ...'

'It's a waterfall,' said Malcolm flatly and there was a silence. How could they find anything that was buried under a waterfall?

'Well,' said Jeffrey after a while, 'there's only one way to find out.'

13

OLD HARRY'S FEET

So it was that on the Friday of Bank Holiday weekend, Malcolm was stashing his bag into the back of Jeffrey's Lada, ready for a trip to Scotland.

It had needed careful handling, but somehow everyone was happy. Jeffrey had been only too pleased to put Ebenezer into service, although it hadn't taken him too long to connect with the idea of Scarface and Scowler.

'These thugs. They're after it too, right? So what happens if they're after us?'

'We just make sure there's no one following us. Anyway, why should they? They've got the waistcoat. They don't know I know anything.'

'Hmmm. I suppose so.'

'Course so. No worries.' Malcolm did however have a few worries of his own. 'Ebenezer's a great car and everything, but, I mean, it will get that far, won't it?'

'In perfect running order—that's what the salesman said.'

'Er, yes. And I mean, it's a long way to drive. I mean, how long ago did you pass your test?'

'Oh ages, three weeks ago now. Looking forward to it—the open road and all that. I need the experience.'

'Er, yes, fine.'

So that was Jeffrey sorted.

Mum was a little harder. 'But the police wanted you to stay indoors.'

'They only said not to walk round Danchester alone. How will I ever get my strength up if I can't get any exercise? Look at my muscles.'

It was true. Malcolm's normally rather weedy physique was exceptionally weedy now.

'Well ... It was kind of Jeffrey to offer to take you. And he is very sensible.'

Jeffrey—sensible? 'Yes, Mum, he'll look after me.'

'You won't do anything dangerous, will you? Climbing mountains or anything?'

'Course not. I promise we won't climb mountains.'

'I'd better tell the police you're going.'

'Oh no ... well, I suppose ... just say we're going on holiday.'

'What else would I say?'

Yes, it would be sensible to tell the police. Malcolm knew that. But they probably wouldn't believe him. Or worse, if they did, they'd say they'd have to be the ones to go and look for it. And it was Malcolm's adventure. He found the clue. He went through all that pain and aggro. After all that he was jolly well going to have the satisfaction of finding it. Or at least having a try.

So it was all arranged. And while Malcolm was loading the Lada, Dad was loading Percy Sedge's Reliant Robin with the waistcoats to sell at the boot fair.

Dad had insisted on finishing the waistcoats himself. It was a matter of pride. He even took up a needle and thread. Finished the embroidery stitches, sewed on buttons. No one in the Crouch household dared giggle.

Dad was definitely getting back to his old self. 'Look here, Malcolm, you're not too hot on corners, you know. Got to make them really sharp. And look at these wonky edges. Attention to detail, that's the key . . .'

'You'll never succeed without it,' muttered Malcolm.

' . . . You'll never succeed without it,' continued Dad.

'Nothing less than excellence,' mumbled Malcolm.

'Excellence, exactly, that's the key. Nothing less than excellence will do.'

But Dad also issued some grudging praise. 'Got to admit though, you've got the edge over me on design. Clothes design, that is. You'd never beat me on an air cooling system, but you've got some good ideas here. When we make the next batch . . .'

We? Was Malcolm hearing right?

' . . . You mastermind design and I'll mastermind production. Pity your mother can't sew.'

'I'll manage finances and marketing,' said Mum coming in with the ironing. 'I've already got one idea. Why don't we call them Walenski's Waistcoats?'

And so it was that on Bank Holiday Saturday morning, Walenski's Waistcoats were selling like hot cakes in the glorious sunshine of Broad Heath Comprehensive car park, and Jeffrey was nosing the Lada through Scottish mist and rain while Malcolm dozed beside him. It was Jeffrey's idea to travel overnight. 'I've been on night shift all week, and beside's there'll be less other traffic.'

He had a point there. As it was they'd been hooted six times and sworn at twice. They'd lost an argument with a concrete bollard, knocked over sixteen traffic cones, and had to back out of a one-way street. They'd been round several roundabouts twice, occasionally to check no one was following, but mostly because they were lost.

But they'd made it, and as Malcolm stretched and yawned, the mist rolled away and the deep blue loch appeared below them, with the grey-green peaks beyond.

'Hey, look,' cried Jeffrey, and pulled over. They both looked, breathing in the stillness with a deep silent 'wow'.

'It's OK up here,' said Malcolm flatly, but his voice had an undertone of awe.

However, there were more urgent needs than peace and serenity. Loos and breakfast first. And then, of course, Old Harry's Seat.

They'd contacted Big Fin before they came. The Adventure Centre was full, he'd explained, and the group would keep him pretty busy. But they could stay in the village with Mrs McPhail and come up Saturday evening—that was his night off.

Mrs McPhail fussed and clucked over them, fed them porridge, bacon, eggs and oatcakes, and showed them to a flowery bedroom with a lingering damp smell and two ancient sagging beds.

'Great, let's get changed and go to Old Harry's Seat,' said Malcolm, but Jeffrey was already sprawled on the bed with his head back and his mouth open. His eyelids fluttered closed and his breathing became heavy and rhythmic.

'Great,' said Malcolm, but he could hardly complain. Jeffrey had chauffeured him all the way there, and if Jeffrey's driving made Malcolm tense, what must it do to Jeffrey?

So Jeffrey slept and Malcolm paced restlessly as the morning passed. After an hour, when Jeffrey's snoring had passed its peak and subsided to a gentle buzz, Malcolm slipped out to the equally drowsy village street. Here and there old ladies paused to chat. Old men leant over gates, watching the lack of passers-by. Malcolm kicked a pebble up the street and felt the tiredness drag at his body. But he was too excited for sleep. Somewhere, under a waterfall, behind a rock, was buried treasure. Not gold or gems but something just as valuable and just as wonderful.

A flapping of wings and harsh cries made Malcolm look up. A flock of geese flew overhead, their calls echoing round the village. *Or it may be just that*, concluded Malcolm—*a wild goose chase*.

He looked down to find himself facing one of Glentalloch's two shops, the newsagents. A map might be handy, he thought, and went in, setting the bell rocking and clanging. It was in the shop that the headline caught his eye: 'Rock star discovered in Scottish hideout'.

> ... *Drongo Leadbitter, the rock star who so mysteriously disappeared six months ago, has been sighted alive and well and living on a Scottish mountain. Locals in the Loch Talloch area say the star has been living in a half-ruined stone cottage in Glen Cuill. He has shunned all friendship, preferring a hermit-like existence in the remote valley* ...

''ere, look at this,' said Scarface, glancing up from his mug of tea.

Scowler continued to examine his fingernails. 'Wot?'

'Old Drongo's turned up in Scotland. They reckon 'e's been there all the time.'

'So?'

'So ... the tape's still not found yet, right? He knows where it is, right? It might even be up there with 'im, right?'

'Right. So?'

'So ... we say, "'allo Drongo old mate, just happened to be in the area. How about a drink for old time's sake?" Or a quick snort, you know what Drongo's like. Get 'im out of 'is skull. "Great idea about the tape, Drongo old son. Where'd you hide it?" 'e talks. Bingo, we find the tape.'

Scowler looked doubtful.

'Or we turn over the place,' continued Scarface. 'There's gotta be some clue.'

Scowler frowned, then brightened. ''e might even have it there with 'im, who knows?'

'Yeah, right, so then, me old mate, I reckon you an me should take a trip to Scotland . . . Well, come on then, no time to waste.'

'Come on.' Malcolm was shaking Jeffrey. 'There's no time to waste. You were right. They've seen him here—Drongo.'

Jeffrey looked blank.

'Oh, come on. It's time we went to Old Harry's Seat.'

It was easy to find the car park by the loch, and easy to find the path to the waterfall. It was an easy walk up the springy, peaty path through the forest, out on to the rocky track, through the narrow valley into the hidden circle of the hills. And there was the place they called Old Harry's Seat. The water thundered down the black slippery rock, tumbling over the edge fifteen metres above, crashing and foaming to the pool below.

After that, nothing was easy.

'Deep beneath Old Harry's feet,' repeated Malcolm. 'It must be at the foot of the waterfall. Come on, Jeffrey, let's go paddling.' Jeffrey still looked dazed, but he took off his shoes and socks as requested and together they waded in. Jeffrey went in a little further downstream than Malcolm—unfortunate, because after two steps he disappeared. A gasping head popped up again. 'I can't . . . I can't . . . He-e-e-e-elp!'

Malcolm stepped in the direction of the snorting wild-eyed head and he too went under as the rock disappeared beneath him.

'I can't swim,' yelled Jeffrey as he was swept away.

151

Malcolm struck out after him, arms and legs flailing in his best crawl—and then discovered, as Jeffrey already had, that the deep pool ended as abruptly as it began.

Jeffrey sat, dripping and sheepish, in the pebbly shallows. Malcolm pulled himself up beside him.

'Good start,' he muttered.

Jeffrey spat out some weed. 'Blessed are those who persevere under trial,' he muttered.

'Let's be scientific about this,' said Malcolm. 'If you're going to put a tape somewhere, you're hardly likely to put it right in the water, are you?'

Jeffrey shook his head.

'So, let's try and find somewhere a bit drier.'

Malcolm was up again, edging carefully around the deep pool, exploring each rock, each nook, each cranny. Jeffrey watched him dolefully, shivering now and again.

'You'll be warmer if you come and help,' said Malcolm, but he took a step backwards as he said it. The water crashed down on his head, the sentence ended in spluttering, and Jeffrey looked unconvinced.

On through the morning, Malcolm searched every possible corner at the base of the waterfall. Every rock, every crack, every tuft of grass, every pebble. In desperation he even stripped to his boxer shorts and dived down to the bottom of the deep pool. Again and again he dived, feeling the rocky surface for something, a box, a cannister, any sort of clue. There was nothing.

Frustrated he surfaced and waded to the bank. A strange sound wafted down from above him. He looked up, and as he did, recognized the sound—giggling. On the ravine's edge above him sat a troop of Girl Guides, eating their sandwiches and clearly enjoying the entertainment. His hands went instinctively to the front of

152

his boxers as he scurried for the bushes. His clothes had disappeared.

The giggling continued unabated and he turned to see why. Jeffrey, stripped too, to his stripey Y-fronts, had taken both his own and Malcolm's clothes and was systematically wringing them out and draping them over the sun-baked rocks to dry. An extra loud giggle made even the oblivious Jeffrey look up. Embarrassed, he turned and grinned at his audience.

'Take a bow, why don't you?' muttered Malcolm from his bush. But Jeffrey had taken the ostrich approach. He lay down on the rock face to dry.

Humiliating or what? thought Malcolm in the shadows. *He's no relative of mine.*

Even a longing for the sun's heat couldn't drag him from his cold hiding place, until the noise of scraping and shuffling and, 'Pick up your litter, gels,' made him realize the Guides were moving off. He emerged shivering from his hiding place, only to hear the tramp of hikers coming up the valley.

'Gee whiz, this place is cute,' said a strident voice.

'Hey, a pool,' said another deeper voice. 'Great place for the picnic.'

'Oh no,' groaned Malcolm, but it was too late to hide.

'Hi,' said the Americans, a middle-aged group dressed, men and women alike, in wide checked shorts, polo shirts, baseball caps, white socks and white and purple trainers.

'Great place you've got here.'

'Er yes,' said Malcolm. Jeffrey had rolled onto his back on the rock. He was smiling and mumbling in his dreams.

'You know, that's a great idea. Why don't we go skinny-dipping?' said a pot-bellied man in a Chicago Bears cap. There was chortled agreement.

Malcolm had had enough. 'Hey, Jeffrey, wake up. It's time we were going.'

Back at Mrs McPhail's, warm, dry and spooning down thick potato and leek broth, they discussed what to do next.

'This Old Harry,' said Jeffrey, looking up from a mildewed guide book he'd found in the ancient parlour, 'how tall d'you suppose he was?'

'What?'

There was a gas fire in the grate and their socks were steaming on the fender. Malcolm stared at the blue flames and decided Jeffrey was definitely out to lunch.

'Well, Old Harry was a giant.'

'If you say so.'

'It says so here. An ancient giant who waded across from Ireland, strode across the mountains and rested at Old Harry's Seat.'

'Yeah, very interesting, Jeffrey.'

'It says you can see his footprints in hollows thirty feet apart across the moors.'

'So?'

'So if his stride was thirty feet, that's at least ten times bigger than us, which means he'd be about sixty feet tall. Now, let's be scientific about this . . .'

'Jeffrey, you don't actually think he was a real person, do you?'

'Well, of course not, but people thought he was. The point is . . .'

'Perhaps you need some more sleep, Jeffrey.'

' . . . the point is, if he was sixty feet tall and he sat at the top of the waterfall, where would his feet be?

Malcolm considered. 'About halfway down.'

'Exactly, so that's where you ought to try.'

'We, Jeffrey,' muttered Malcolm. 'That's where we're gonna try.'

They trudged back up the hillside in the late afternoon. The sun was lower already and the bracken gave off a warm, dry smell. They were ready for every eventuality this time. Swimming shorts underneath, boots and waterproofs on top. Malcolm carried the Lada's new blue tow rope. Jeffrey inexplicably had brought a spanner.

At the foot of the waterfall they stopped to look up. About halfway down the water bounced and crashed off a ledge of rock. It seemed possible that behind the curtain of water was a narrow dry gap. It even seemed possible you could walk along it.

'Yes!' yelled Malcolm and leapt on Jeffrey as if he'd just scored a goal. Jeffrey looked embarrassed but pleased.

'And see, up there. There's a narrow little path, winds down from the top. I'm sure it goes to the ledge. Come on, let's go to the top of the waterfall.'

They made their way back down the valley till they found the track to the top of the ravine. The hills closed in to form a cliff around the top of the valley. Jeffrey looked over once and gulped. He stayed away after that and kept his face stiffly ahead. At the head of the valley they found the stream rushing merrily down a gentle slope before plunging over the edge. They picked their way across it, leaping from rock to rock, till they got to the point where the little path seemed to start. A barricade of fencing and barbed wire met their gaze.

'Danger, rock fall,' said a sign. 'Keep away.' Malcolm leaned over to see as best he could. True enough, a sheer drop of about four metres gave way to a slide of rubble beneath. The sign looked quite recent.

'Ah,' said Malcolm. Strangers certainly didn't go there now. If they ever did.

Jeffrey, after his giant burst of inspiration, was silent once more, nervously keeping away from the edge. Malcolm nosed around, peering over, scrambling down one side of the ravine to examine the ledge.

'There's definitely a gap behind the water, he called. 'I'm sure you could walk along it . . . But you just can't get there.'

He sighed and looked up to the top of the fall. In the centre one large jagged rock protruded, parting the waters each side of it. Malcolm stared at it for a while, looked up and down, up and down and then returned to Jeffrey with a determined look.

'How'd you like to play at being a giant, Jeffrey? How'd you like to sit on Old Harry's Seat?'

Jeffrey panicked, argued, whinged, pleaded, but Malcolm was determined.

'We haven't come this far for nothing. You've only got to sit there and lower the rope when I say. If you sit astride that outcrop, you can't possibly fall. The worse you'll get is a wet bum. Come on, Jeffrey. Just think, there's treasure down there. Well, there might be.'

Jeffrey looked doubtful. 'The Bible says we should lay up treasure in heaven, Malcolm. I'm not sure if this is right for me, you know.'

Even so, he couldn't quite resist Malcolm's excitement.

'What if you slip?' he asked.

'The rope will hold me.'

'What if the rope slips?'

'It won't, we'll wrap it round the rock.'

'What if it breaks?'

'Jeffrey, it's strong enough to pull cars.'

'Yes, but what if . . .?'

156

'Even if I fell, there's that deep pool below. I'd just dive in.'

'But what if *I* fell?'

'You can't fall, honest. Jeffrey, come on!'

With that last impassioned plea, Malcolm dragged Jeffrey to his post. Jeffrey's face was ever whiter as he picked his way over slippery rocks and gushing water, ever nearer to the edge. Malcolm shoved him into position.

'Sit on the rock, there, and put your legs astride it. Great. Now shuffle forward.'

The rock jutted out over the edge like a giant saddle. A jagged peak in the centre acted as a pommel.

'Great. Don't look . . . No, don't.' But Jeffrey had made the mistake of looking down. His head shot back with a shudder.

'You're quite safe,' repeated Malcolm. 'It's me that's got the hairy bit,' he muttered to himself. 'Now, tie the rope round the rock, like so. Now loop it round the peak.' Malcolm wrapped the other end round his waist. 'All you have to do, when I say, is to let the rope out, like this. When I'm down there, just hold it steady.'

Jeffrey's eyes were closed. He seemed to be praying.

'Did you hear what I said?'

'Yes, yes. Let the rope out . . . Malcolm, are you sure it's safe? What will I tell Uncle Bob and Auntie Cathy if . . .'

'Tell them it's all my fault. Now—just hold on, Jeffrey. That's all you need to do.'

Malcolm, stripped to shorts, T-shirt and boots, lowered himself over the edge of the waterfall. Immediately he swung inwards. The gushing water took his breath away, and for a moment he almost released his grip. He spluttered for a moment and steadied himself, pushing away with his feet. 'Now, Jeffrey,' he yelled. 'Lower me down.'

Jeffrey, eyes tight closed, let out the rope. Malcolm, eyes blinking against the spray, put his feet through the water and on to the rock and edged his way down. He had a feeling that Big Fin wouldn't approve of this technique. He looked below. The ledge still seemed far away. The pool looked like Guinness, deep brown below the white foam. Malcolm hung there, on the flimsy evidence of a scrap of paper, and he was praying too.

Somehow, after a sickening eternity, his feet touched the ledge. The water, like a pounding, deafening sheet was in front of him. There was nothing for it. He ducked under.

After he'd stopped choking, coughing and spluttering, Malcolm found himself in a secret cave-like world. The ledge was a little less than a metre wide, the cliff overhanging it and the water falling straight down like a booming curtain.

It was a damp, secret place, strangely still behind the noise. Malcolm wiped his eyes and looked around him. Across the sparkling water was a rainbow. A rainbow that danced. It changed as you looked at it, from one angle to another, now bright, now subtle, but it was a rainbow that never went away.

'Ah,' said Malcolm. He was beginning to understand. But there was work to do. He turned his attention to the rock behind him. He did not have to look far. At about head height was a narrow lip of rock, behind it was a gap, a crack in the rock, only wide enough for a man's hand. Malcolm put his hand in. Felt to the right, nothing there. Felt to the left, something, a package, wedged tightly in the crack. Malcolm tugged and tugged. If only his fingers were longer. If only his nails weren't bitten down. If only he had a . . .

Excited, he launched himself out beyond the watery curtain.

'Jeffrey,' he yelled, 'I've found it.'

Jeffrey's ashen face appeared over the edge.

'But I can't get it out. I'm going to untie myself. When I do, pull the rope up and tie the spanner on. Good thinking, the spanner, by the way. Sorry I was rude about it. Anyway, tie it on and lower it down.'

It seemed a good idea at the time. But as Malcolm stood inside the curtain, as near the edge as he dared, and the spanner hung tantalizingly out of reach outside it, he realized the snag.

'Swing it, Jeffrey,' he yelled hopelessly. 'Swing it in, then I might catch it.'

Whether Jeffrey heard, or worked the problem out for himself, Malcolm never found out, but the spanner started swinging, back and forth like a pendulum, now just touching the curtain of water, now nearly through.

'More, Jeffrey,' yelled Malcolm. 'More.'

Could he have seen above him, he would have realized what he was asking. In order to get the momentum it needed, Jeffrey was half standing, leaning far out over the waterfall, steadying himself with one hand while swinging the rope with the other. His face had the grim determination of someone about to meet the firing squad.

The Girl Guides, trooping wearily back downhill, gawped in amazement. 'Come on, gels. Don't stare. Just some harmless lunatic.'

The harmless lunatic waved a spanner on the end of a rope over a waterfall and yelled to someone unseen, 'I'm doing my best, Malc. I'm doing my best.'

The spanner kept swinging like a pendulum, and the last Guide had just disappeared over the crest of the hill when a hand shot half through the waterfall to grab it.

Malcolm, soaking, shivering and weak at the knees, grabbed the spanner. He didn't bother to untie it, just thrust it into the crack and levered it under the package. He levered it up and down, pushed and pulled and . . .

The box came free.

The spanner jerked away. The box fell out. Malcolm made a grab for it. He caught it, but his foot hit a slippery patch and he reeled backwards. For a slow-motion moment he struggled to keep his balance. And then he was over, tumbling and bumping down the rocks. Gasping and choking, but not letting go of the box.

He landed, bruised but intact, in the pool. *I made it,* he thought, and then realized that the boots on his feet and the box in his hand made it impossible to swim the few strokes to safety. He went under gurgling and his feet touched the bottom. With a strength derived from panic, he pushed himself up. He surfaced briefly, enough for him to lift an arm and throw the box to the bank. Then he was under again, fighting against it, feeling the strength drain from him. He pushed feebly with all his last energy, his arms flailed wildly. His lungs, his poor damaged lungs felt as if they would burst. There was no strength left.

Then he hit the shelf of rock.

He pulled himself up, slowly edging forward, until he lay gasping in a muddy puddle. He felt as if he would never move again, but a noise made him look up. Jeffrey, still astride Old Harry's Seat, was talking to himself. 'Praise the Lord in all things. Fear not, fear not. Don't panic. He-e-elp! Help me someone, I'm stuck!'

14

EBENEZER'S REVENGE

It was an unimpressive treasure chest—a plastic sand-wich box taped round the seal—but on it was written, smudged but unmistakeable, 'Silent Music'.

They were up at the Adventure Centre now, grateful to borrow some dry clothes from Big Fin and watch their second wet set of the day steaming around another fire.

'I'll say this for you, Malcolm,' said Big Fin, familiar bottled beer in hand. 'You've got no sense, but you're certainly determined.' He turned to Jeffrey. 'And you. Took some guts, eh?'

'And he figured where to look,' added Malcolm.

Jeffrey swelled visibly, 'But come on then, let's open the jolly thing. We may as well hear it.'

With fumbling fingers Malcolm pulled the tape off. Inside were several layers of black plastic and inside that a lining of what felt like small linen sandbags.

'Silica gel,' said Jeffrey. 'Absorbs moisture.'

Inside them was another box and inside that was a tape. Thoughts of playing it disappeared: this was no normal cassette—similar but smaller and squarer. No matter—it was definitely a tape.

'Silent Music,' said the label. 'Leadbitter Riff—master copy.'

On a large green sheet of paper tucked into the box was a letter:

Dear Finder
Congratulations, whoever you are. This recording and all rights and profits are yours. Take it to my legal adviser—J.M.P. McCauley, 3 Crown Street, London EC1—and he will do the rest.
Enjoy the dosh. May it do good to you, and may you do good with it. Better than me and Riff anyway. There's more to life than money, more to life than success. They all tell you, but you never believe it until it's too late. It was too late for Riff anyway. Maybe it's not too late for me.
Enjoy the music. I hope you do. It's classic Leadbitter Riff, all except the last track. I wrote 'Silent Music' myself. It's not that good, not without Riff, he always had the best tunes. It's my tribute to him—to the music he'll never make now, the music he'll never hear.
Our heads got so full of noise. We were swept along in the stream. Faster and faster. Speed to get us going, booze to blank it out.
Performing's a drug in itself. It's great, really great, but where are you when you come down?
You get carried along in it all. And if you're not careful you go over the edge. Riff did.
I got out in time. I always felt that above the noise there was some other music. Some silent music I wasn't hearing. You catch it now and then, or it catches you. I caught it once when I was a kid. About thirteen or so, and we came here to Scotland in a caravan. I was bored—I couldn't bring my guitar—except one day I went behind the waterfall. I was in the stillness behind the noise. There was a curtain between me and the world. There were rainbows there. You could only see them in the secret place.

*So I've been trying to catch the music. Maybe one day. I
haven't given up yet.*
Peace,
Drongo

Big Fin twirled his beer bottle, watching the flames
change shape behind it.

'What he needs is to meet the Musician,' he said.
'Hope he finds what he's looking for.'

'He's been seen round here,' said Malcolm, after a
pause. 'That's how we guessed, 'cos Jeffrey met him.'

'Sharing the gospel,' added Jeffrey with modest
pride.

'Yup,' said Big Fin, 'over in the Cuill valley, they say,
old McIntosh's place.'

'You knew,' gasped Malcolm.

Big Fin nodded. 'Fella's entitled to his own life. If he
wanted to be alone, good luck to him.'

'He won't be alone for long,' said Malcolm. It's in the
papers now.' He explained the report he'd glimpsed in
the newsagents.

'He'll be gone then,' said Big Fin, poking at a log on
the fire. 'He'll be travelling already, I reckon.'

'Oh,' said Malcolm. He hunched his shoulders.

Big Fin looked at him and smiled. 'The lad's got a fortune at his fingertips and he looks like he's been left
holding a sheep's turd.'

'It's just that . . . well, I'd love to meet him and tell
him I found "Silent Music".'

'Too late now, I reckon.'

'But how does he know? If he's a hermit, he'll hardly
have popped out for the papers.' Jeffrey's logic came as a
jolt. His closed eyes and open mouth gave the impression that he was out of the conversation.

'True,' admitted Big Fin.

163

'I know, why don't we go and warn him? Just say hello and warn him. Maybe we can help him escape.'

'Escape? Come on, Malcolm, you've been watching too many stupid adventure films,' said Jeffrey.

'Look,' said Malcolm, 'not even the stupidest films have rock albums hidden behind waterfalls. Escaping from the press seems perfectly logical to me.'

'It'll take them a while to find him.' said Big Fin thoughtfully. 'It'd be a kindness to warn him. I'd go myself, but the lads are back soon. Why don't you go? It's sixteen kilometres as the crow flies, about sixty by road.

'Take the single track up over Ben Carroch. Go through the gate at the cattle grid, make sure you close it again. Bit of a hairpin on the way down, great views, watch the drop though. Take it gentle on the bend, there's many a tourist gone over into the loch. Five miles on from the "road narrows" sign, there's the turning for the valley. When the road stops you keep on up the track, watch for the ruts. When you can go no further, you'll see a tumbledown white cottage under some trees.'

'Got that, Jeffrey?' asked Malcolm.

'You'll not make it before dark though.'

Jeffrey, whey-faced and trembling a little, was suddenly decisive. 'Tomorrow,' he said firmly. 'I've had enough for one day.'

They sat round the fire a little longer, watching it glow and die. Big Fin raked the embers and the sparks leapt out. *He looks tired*, thought Malcolm, noticing him properly for the first time.

'Busy week, Fin?'

He smiled. 'Hard work. Lads from Kilgarvie Retraining Establishment—borstal it was in my day. Yobbos basically, but then I was one once. They think they're hard men, gotta keep trying to prove it. Soft as butter underneath.'

'It's a fine work,' said Jeffrey piously. 'The Lord will surely bless.'

'He'd better get on with it then. Government cutbacks. No grants. Trustees threatening to close us. We're a luxury, these days. But we're clinging on.'

'The Lord will provide,' said Jeffrey.

'Tell that to my lads with no jobs,' snapped Big Fin. Then he sighed. 'You're right. Something always turns up.'

The deep silence was broken by the sound of engines. Two minibuses roared into the compound and died away. Another noise replaced them, almost musical, coming nearer:

'We're the barmy rangers army,' and 'If you're looking for a fight, 'ere we are' echoed around the huts and made it clear that the lads had come back from a night on the town.

'Well, we'll be going then,' said Jeffrey nervously. 'Come on, Malcolm, early start tomorrow.'

But Malcolm was fast asleep.

It wasn't that early a start. A good night's sleep was a far greater attraction than they realized and it was nearly eleven as they bumped up the Cuill valley track, stomachs still groaning under Mrs McPhail's breakfast. A map and Big Fin's instructions had done the trick and before them sure enough was the white half-derelict cottage surrounded by tall pines.

'Stop here,' said Malcolm suddenly. 'We don't want to frighten him off.'

Malcolm picked his way up the dirt track and pushed the gate. It hung from one hinge and scraped the ground. Malcolm had the feeling of being on hallowed ground. Jeffrey merely felt like a trespasser.

There was no sign of life. No dog barking, no limp

washing on a line, no boots in a porch. Their knock sounded thin and flat, but the air around was so still you felt that even a mouse squeak would have carried.

They tried again. Nothing. Getting bolder, Malcolm banged on a window. Louder now, no one could miss it. But no one came.

Malcolm peered in. Dusty dried flowers met his gaze, beyond them a bare corridor leading to a sunlit kitchen. Cups and plates stacked in the drying rack, a pot plant in need of the last rites, the fridge door hanging open.

They made their way round the back, past the crumbling stable, and stones that were once an outhouse. A spider's web hung across the kitchen door. The grass was long and untrodden. They peered through every window and keyhole. They were still round the back when they heard the noise of traffic.

Traffic? They ran to the side of the garden to see a strange cavalcade in slow procession up the valley. In front was a taxi, behind it a jeep with a tall aerial coming from the top. Behind that was a row of assorted cars, two motorcycles and some small boys on bikes.

They drew to a dusty halt. Out climbed men with furry microphones on poles, men with TV cameras hoisted on their shoulders. Women with smaller cameras with huge long lenses. Men and women with tape machines and notebooks.

As Malcolm and Jeffrey came round the house there was a gentle clicking and whirring of cameras. It soon stopped as what seemed like the the entire world's press glared accusingly at Malcolm and Jeffrey.

'There's no one here,' said Malcolm. 'Not as far as I can see.'

'He's gone,' added Jeffrey.

'Who's gone?' asked a woman with a thrusting microphone.

'Er, no one. I mean, whoever was here isn't here now.'

'Is it right that Drongo Leadbitter lives here?' asked a tall man with a drooping moustache.

'Who?' said Jeffrey, a picture of naïvety.

'Come on,' said a reporter. 'Everyone knows Drongo Leadbitter.'

'You don't know my cousin Jeffrey,' said Malcolm.

'Look, we know he's here.'

'You mean Drongo Leadbitter lives here?' Malcolm's voice rose in innocent awe.

'It's what we've been told. What are you doing here?'

'Lost, went the wrong way. Jeffrey's driving. Needed a loo,' explained Malcolm. 'Come on Jeffrey, we're going to be really late.'

'Late for what?'

'Just late.' Malcolm kicked him. 'Come on.'

The photographers were setting up in bushes when Malcolm and Jeffrey left. Reporters were talking down mobile phones to their editors, and the film crew was paying off the taxi driver. Malcolm turned for a last look at the blank cottage. The lower branches of pine whispered against the dormer windows. Their thick panes looked beyond to meadow, moors and distant mountains. He hoped, with a sudden pang in his stomach, that Drongo had been happy here.

Jeffrey was just completing a 23-point turn in the lane when the taxi came down empty. The driver leaned out conspiratorially. 'He's not here, you know. He's gone. Took him to the station mesel' on Friday. They're in for a long wait.' He chuckled.

'How did they find out where he was?' asked Malcolm as Jeffrey made graunching noises with the gears.

'Oh, I told 'em. After he'd gone. For a price. Made more in this week than I make in a year.' He was still chuckling as he drove off.

As they drove down the lane, other cars kept coming up.

'Poor guy. I'm glad he has gone.' said Malcolm. 'If I was him, I'd disappear.'

They were just at the crossroads when another car came up. It was an old blue Cortina and the occupants were strangely familiar. They paused and stared for a moment before turning up the lane to the Cuill Valley.

'It's them!' said Malcolm. 'Follow that car!'

'Who?' said Jeffrey, stepping on the brakes and turning to look at the same time. The car drew to a screeching halt in a hedgerow.

'Them. The ones who attacked me. Come on, follow them.'

Jeffrey looked in his mirror. 'I don't think I need to. I think they're following me.'

Sure enough, the Cortina was reversing back down the lane. It was turning.

Malcolm felt sick. He remembered pain—falling down and a searing pain in his chest. 'Come on, get away from them. They've got knives. They've probably got guns. Drive like crazy.'

The Lada squealed up the road with a smell of rubber. The Cortina completed its turn and lurched behind.

'Where are we going?' asked Jeffrey, his knuckles white on the wheel.

'Dunno, anywhere. Just so they don't get us.'

'I don't think I'll lose them. Ebenezer's a good car, but...'

'Not that good,' agreed Malcolm. 'Just keep going. Don't let them get in front.'

They had never been more grateful for single-track roads. Jeffrey stayed in the middle and blasted the hooter every time they came to a bend.

'They must think we know something,' said Jeffrey.

'We do,' said Malcolm.

'They think we've got the tape,' said Jeffrey.

'We have,' said Malcolm. *The tape! Where was it?* He'd fallen asleep last night in front of Big Fin's fire, the tape in the picnic box at his side. 'Where's the tape?'

'Safe,' said Jeffrey, teeth gritted at he tackled a tight bend.

'Safe where?'

'In a safe. In Big Fin's safe at the Adventure Centre.'

'Watch out!' The hedge came up to meet them and Jeffrey just swerved in time. A rough scraping sound ran down the side of the car.

'Just drive, don't talk,' said Malcolm.

'Don't ask questions,' said Jeffrey. 'Oh no!'

Ahead of them the lane was filled by a huge continental coach.

'Hold on,' said Jeffrey. 'I think we'll do it.'

Malcolm closed his eyes as they drove straight for the coach. He felt a swerve and heard a harsh scraping, the other side of the car this time. He opened his eyes to find the coach gone. He turned to see astonished French tourists gaping back at him. Somewhere, stuck behind the coach was the Cortina.

'Passing place,' explained Jeffrey, 'sort of.'

Malcolm discovered he was trembling.

'Given them the slip. Nifty, eh?' said Jeffrey.

He was so pleased with himself he failed to notice the stop sign at the cross roads. He screeched to a halt in the middle, reversed and turned right. 'Mountain road. They'll never know we went this way. Brilliant, eh?'

'Brilliant, Jeffrey.'

And suddenly they were alone in the wide silent moorland, a dot on a vast landscape, crawling up the mountain road. Jeffrey flexed his tense knuckles and grinned. 'You know, I rather enjoyed that. I've always fancied being in a car chase.'

'Too many rubbishy films,' said Malcolm.

'No,' said Jeffrey seriously, 'books. *The Thirty-nine Steps.*'

Shadows raced over the heather. Curlews rose squawking. Idly, Malcolm looked back. Far below, a blue Cortina was coming up the hairpin mountain road.

'Jeffrey, you know you said you liked car chases.'

'Mmm.'

'Well, we're still in one. Step on it!'

'I am stepping on it,' said Jeffrey, as they crawled up the hill.

At the bend it was even steeper. The Lada stalled. Malcolm watched the Cortina get nearer and bigger.

'Come on, come on,' muttered Malcolm as Ebenezer turned over sluggishly.

'Come on, old thing,' said Jeffrey, turning the ignition once more. 'It needs a certain touch.'

'More like a miracle, I'd say,' said Malcolm.

'You're right!' Jeffrey stopped and closed his eyes. 'Dear Lord, we do beseech you to hear your children now in their hour of need and send forth your . . .'

'What he means is "Help"!' said Malcolm.

Jeffrey tried again. The engine burst into glorious life and they crawled upward once more. And then they were on the top. Racing along on top of the world, sheep pausing from their munching to watch them pass. Malcolm glanced back. The Cortina could not be far behind but for the moment it was still climbing, hidden from view.

'Oh no,' Jeffrey groaned.

Malcolm turned again. The gate. They'd forgotten the gate. The Cortina was coming over the horizon behind them.

Jeffrey was still accelerating. 'When I slow right down,' he said, 'jump out and open the gate. And whatever you do, make sure you shut it again.'

'Now,' he yelled. Malcolm ran for the gate. The Cortina was gaining every minute, it was metres away as he fumbled with the catch. He opened it and Jeffrey roared through. Scarface was leaping from the Cortina. *Wasn't that something in his hand?* For a second Malcolm paused, yearning to leave the gate swinging and run for the safety of the car. 'Close it,' yelled Jeffrey. Numbly Malcolm pushed the gate, aware of Scarface coming nearer and of his own unprotected flesh.

Must shut it. Must shut it. Done.

For a moment his eyes met Scarface's glare. No one said a word. Then he was running, Ebenezer was revving, and they were away. Malcolm looked back. Scarface, empty-handed, was fumbling with the gate.

A gamekeeper out on the moors saw the two ancient cars racing downhill. 'Flamin' tourists. I'd shoot the lot of them.' He aimed a pot shot at the yellow leader. It glanced off the boot.

'They *have* got a gun,' gasped Malcolm.

'Just a pebble,' said Jeffrey.

They were approaching the main road. People, other cars, civilization. Safety at last. But suddenly Jeffrey was turning off, taking the forest road to the Adventure Centre.

'What the...? Jeffrey, what're you doing? This road's a dead end. We'll never get away!'

'I'm not trying to,' said Jeffrey. 'I'm making sure they don't get away from us.'

As he passed through the stockade into the Adventure Centre, Jeffrey hit the horn. He circled around the cabins, hooter blaring and the Cortina followed him in. He brought the Lada to a halt, sideways on, blocking the entrance to the stockade. Then he sat and waited. The Cortina screeched to a stop. Scarface and Scowler looked around, puzzled, at the empty compound. They got out and approached the Lada.

'Lock your door,' said Jeffrey.

Malcolm locked it. He sank in his seat as Scarface and Scowler strode menacingly towards the Lada.

And then from the dining cabin, Big Fin appeared. Other figures followed him—large menacing figures. Skinheads with scars. Longhairs with tattoos and nose-rings. Guys in T-shirts that said 'Nazi Power', and 'Smash the System', and 'Celtic Forever'. Guys who smashed their fists together ready for a fight. Big Fin held up his hand and they stood in a circle waiting.

Jeffrey got out of the car and approached Scarface and Scowler.

'Did you want something?' he said.

15

MONEY MATTERS

By the time all the explanations were over, the sun was slipping down behind the ridge. Scarface and Scowler had been taken off down the hill in the police van—charged with GBH and theft of two waistcoats. They'd admitted it, or at least Scowler had by trying to deny it.

'I never meant to kill him, honest. I only wanted to frighten him and get the waistcoat off him. The knife just slipped. Honest, what d'you take me for? I don't mind taking out villains, I wouldn't go for an innocent kid.'

He looked so guilty that Malcolm almost felt sorry for him. But mostly he felt an enormous and unexpected burst of relief when they were finally handcuffed and taken away. He was tired, he realized, deadly, deadly tired. It was all over and he stupidly felt like crying.

As the van drove off, Malcolm slipped away to sit by the stream. He watched as, moment by moment, the sun disappeared behind the mountain. He was still sitting there in the darkness when a familiar glow told him that Big Fin was coming. Big Fin sat down beside him and drew on his cigarette.

'The lads enjoyed that,' he said. 'Made their day, someone else getting nicked for a change.'

'Oh, good,' said Malcolm vaguely.

'Jeffrey's playing pool with the lads. He said he wanted to get conversant with modern youth culture. He'll get some interesting culture from that lot.'

'Uh-huh,' said Malcolm.

'So how's things at home these days?'

'Oh!' Malcolm was surprised Big Fin remembered. 'Bit better, I suppose. Although now . . .' Malcolm brightened. 'With the money, I mean . . .' He began to think. 'It'll be thousands, won't it. Millions, even. Dad won't need to work. Nor Mum. We can get a telly and a video. And a new car. I'll get a mega sound system. We can go on holiday. It'll be one long holiday. Wow, we could get a posh house. Dunno about that, Mum'd be really fussy. Or a villa in Spain. I'll get some fantastic new clothes, even get Stacey some. A sailing boat, new mountain bike, tons of CDs . . .'

'Hmmm,' said Big Fin. 'Be careful. Money does funny things to people.'

'What sort of funny?'

'Look at Drongo and Riff.'

'So?' said Malcolm defensively.

The stream gurgled, the trees rustled and Big Fin just shrugged.

'Well, anyway,' said Malcolm. 'We haven't got it yet.'

'I'm afraid getting hold of the money may not be that easy.' J.M.P. McCauley peered over his half-moon glasses.

Dad, Malcolm and Jeffrey shifted uneasily on their velvet chairs. The discreet grandeur of the solicitors' office made you feel they were charging you to sit there.

'Leadbitter Riff's management will contest it. They're very angry with Drongo and his antics. They claim there's a clause in the contract giving them authority over copyright details.'

'And is there?'

'Well, it's hard to say. It would have to go to the courts. I believe they do have a case. If you'll allow me to . . .'

'You mean they'd ignore what Drongo said?'

'They'll claim it was a statement made under extreme emotional pressure.'

'And take the money themselves?' Malcolm bounced on his chair in annoyance.

'They can't actually do that,' said J.M.P. McCauley, twirling his fingers round his thinning grey ponytail. 'But they can hold it until he reappears. It would be a tidy sum to underwrite their other ventures. But if you'll allow me to represent you, I believe we can fight it.'

'How long would it take?'

'Oh, no more than a couple of years. Unless there's an appeal.'

'It would cost a fortune, wouldn't it? Who'd pay you?'

'Well, of course, I'd be prepared to defer payment until you won the case. Then it could come out of the rights.'

'And if we didn't win?'

'Well, of course, there'd still be some charges to pay. I'd try to keep them to a minimum, but . . .'

'How do we know,' Dad narrowed his eyes suspiciously, 'that you're not in with them?'

J.M.P. McCauley laughed, a thin dribble of a laugh. 'Now really, I can assure you I have Drongo's best interests at heart. I'm one of the few people around him who's not after his money.' He leaned forward conspiratorially. 'You know who hired your two muggers? Linda Lacey.'

Only Malcolm's face showed any comprehension. 'Really? Drongo's girlfriend.'

'Ex-girlfriend,' said J.M.P. McCauley. 'Frightful gold-digger. Didn't care that Drongo was going off and leaving her. All she cared about was that he left her the mansion in Surrey and a fat monthly allowance. He didn't, so she hired those unsavoury characters. He'd got her to dump a pile of his clothes in an Oxfam collection box, you see. She started being suspicious when she realized his favourite waistcoat was missing—she sussed the rainbow connection. Got them searching every Oxfam shop for miles. Police won't get her. She's in South America now.

'But your question. If you're really worried, you could take on another solicitor to represent yourselves.'

'And how would we afford that?' muttered Dad. He took up the sandwich box which lay on the wide leather-topped desk between them.

'Mr Crouch, please. Mr Crouch. That tape is immensely valuable. Now why don't you let me look after it. If you'll let me represent you . . .'

Dad got up to go.

' . . . Mr Crouch! It really ought to be held in safe keeping.'

'It is,' said Dad. 'Mine. Come on, boys. We'll be in touch in due course.'

He was heading for the door.

Malcolm and Jeffrey sat gloomily in the sandwich bar. It was early for lunch, but they'd caught the 7.15 for London and now they were hungry. But nothing tasted good. They chewed their Danish pastries and sipped their milk shakes, but what ought to have been a great day out had gone definitely unmistakeably sour.

After the disastrous meeting with the solicitor, Dad had gone off. 'Errands to do,' he said mysteriously. 'See you at four o'clock.'

'Can't believe my Dad,' said Malcolm. 'We've just lost a fortune and he doesn't seem bothered.'

'The Lord gives and the Lord takes away,' said Jeffrey. 'All things work together for good, you know, Malcolm.'

Malcolm stopped mid-slurp and slowly and deliberately took the straw from his milkshake. He raised the glass to his eyes.

'Jeffrey,' he said, 'shut up. If you quote just one more stupid bit of religion at me, I'll pour this chocolate milkshake all over your head.'

Jeffrey looked aggrieved. He shut up. They continued to slurp and munch in uncomfortable silence.

Malcolm began to feel guilty. 'I don't mind if you believe it,' he said grudgingly after a while. 'But why'd you have to go on about it so much?'

'Perhaps I do go on a bit,' Jeffrey admitted, so shamefaced that Malcolm almost felt sorry for him. 'But when Christ came into my life it changed me.'

'Yeah, it made you boring,' said Malcolm crossly.

'Oh, well, I always thought I was pretty boring anyway.'

Malcolm thought about it. Yeah, Jeffrey had always been one of life's anoraks. Before it was religion it was bird-watching, and before that it was model railways. You could hardly blame him, mind, with a mother like Auntie May. After Uncle Bert died (Malcolm vaguely remembered a thin sad-faced man), Auntie May had 'gone to pieces'. That was what Mum said. She was already old when she had Jeffrey and now he was all she had to fuss over. If there were diplomas in fussing, Auntie May would have one. So Jeffrey had to wear warm vests and have neatly-parted hair and be in by ten o'clock—and that was after he was eighteen and she started letting him out at nights on his own. *Fancy knowing you were boring*, thought Malcolm.

'Sorry, I didn't mean it,' said Malcolm, 'about you being boring.'

'Oh well, I always thought it, 'cos I never had many friends. You know, what with Mum always wanting me home. Not till I met those church people. They were so friendly. They didn't seem to think I was too odd. They invited me along, so I went. It was the first time I ever felt I belonged anywhere.'

'Yeah, well, that's very nice for you . . . Doesn't mean you can ram it at everyone though.'

'No, no, but it's not just that. You see, one day I prayed, like they said to, and it worked.'

'What d'you mean, it worked?'

'I mean, I mean, what I mean is—it was like I really belonged—to God. It's hard to explain. You see, the Bible says, "To all who receive him, he gives power to become the sons of God." Think of that! Jesus said, "I am come that they might have life in all its fullness." Well, my life's getting fuller. It's like St Paul says . . .'

Jeffrey broke off. He took the chocolate milkshake and solemnly poured it over his head.

'Save you doing it,' he said.

Office workers ordering baguettes and bagels stared mystified as chocolate trickled down Jeffrey's ears and dripped on to his lilac and turquoise track suit. Malcolm sat open-mouthed.

The man behind the counter spat out a stream of angry words. They didn't sound like English, but the last ones were clear enough. 'Get outta my café.'

'I think he thinks you're a weirdo,' said Malcolm as they left the sandwich bar. He found a grubby hanky to wipe Jeffrey down. 'But as weirdos go, you're not so bad.'

Jeffrey wiped his glasses with a tissue. 'You see, no one would take notice of what *I* say. That's why I quote the Bible.'

'It sounds better when you say it,' said Malcolm. 'Just telling what happened.'

'Oh,' Jeffrey smiled. 'You don't think it sounds too weird then?'

'No,' said Malcolm. 'It sounds OK.'

Then in this day of surprises, Jeffrey had another one. 'Let's go to Madame Tussaud's. I'll pay.'

Jeffrey, renowned for his stinginess, was paying for some fun!

Another discovery: Jeffrey could be funny. He draped himself alongside Joan Collins, shook hands with the Pope, and sat still on a bench for so long that an Arab lady nearly fainted when he moved. They were laughing so much they almost forgot to meet Dad.

They found him under a lion in Trafalgar Square, pacing backwards and forwards with a huge smile on his face. He waved a piece of paper.

'Hey, our first order,' he bellowed and all around pigeons flapped upwards. 'Walenski's Waistcoats. They ordered thirty in La Bella and two dozen in Blanes. Frightfully posh, they were. They said they were impressed with the excellent quality and attention to detail. Now, how about a milkshake?'

Dad was so elated he brought cream cakes all round.

'It was Mrs Walenski's idea,' he explained. 'Trying Knightsbridge boutiques. She suggested La Bella. They put me on to Blanes.'

'But, Dad,' reminded Malcolm, 'We can't even afford the material. We're still broke. No fortune, remember.'

'Trust in the . . .' said Jeffrey, then stopped.

'No problem,' said Dad, 'That was my other errand. I went to the record company. Told them we had the tape. Didn't tell them it was in my carrier bag. Thought they

179

might mug me! Anyway, they're desperate to get their hands on it. They've offered us £100,000.'

Malcolm and Jeffrey opened their mouths and the straws dropped down in unison.

'Well,' said Dad modestly, 'They offered us £40,000 at first and I beat them up to £100,000. We don't get the rights, but it's better than nothing. I said I'd have to ask you first.'

Malcolm and Jeffrey's grins showed that it was indeed better than nothing.

'They say the whole story will be great publicity. And it will, it'll be great publicity for Walenski's Waistcoats.'

16

WALENSKI'S WORKSHOP

Outside No. 27 Lavinia Close, a pack of journalists, TV crews and photographers was camped on the pavement.

Inside, the Crouch family was in conference.

It had come, the sort of cheque you want to frame; and the tape, sandwich box and all, had been ceremoniously handed over to Groundhog Recordings.

'They're all arguing,' said Dad, 'J.M.P. McCauley, Rockface Management, Linda Lacey and Groundhog. Loads of solicitors, all sending each other rude letters. They've tried writing to us, but I sent the letters back. All we did was hand over some lost property and happen to get a reward. Not our problem.'

'That lot outside are,' said Mum. 'They're even asking for cups of tea.'

'Forget tea, woman,' said Dad cheerfully. 'You're our finance director and marketing manager. Sit down, for goodness sake. Let 'em wait.'

They sat round the dining table, Dad, Malcolm and Mum. Dad cleared his throat impressively and began.

'This cheque, of course, is Malcolm's property, but since he is a minor the bulk of it will go into a trust fund to be held until he attains his legal majority.'

'Your eighteenth birthday, love,' explained Mum.

'That's stupid,' muttered Malcolm. 'What's the point of it just sitting there all those years?'

'However,' continued Dad, 'I believe Malcolm has indicated his willingness to advance a proportion of the sum—let's say, £10,000—as a start up loan to Walenski's Waistcoats, the money to be paid back into the trust, with interest if possible, over a period of five years. You, Malcolm, will be a non-executive director, Mrs Walenski and I will be directors and Mum will be company secretary.'

Mum beamed. 'That's not just a secretary who does typing,' she explained. 'It's the person who runs all the business side.'

'The bulk of the loan will go into hiring premises and equipment,' explained Dad.

'And a computer course for me,' added Mum.

'. . . We'll employ people on piece-work at first. Peggy from Peggy's Fabrics has suggested some good workers. And Percy from next door has asked if he can learn the trade. He's a first-class worker. Mrs Walenski says he's learning fast. I'd like Malcolm to work on the design side, along with Mrs Walenski—but, of course, school work must come first.

Malcolm sighed. *This was all my idea in the first place*, he grumbled to himself. *Dad's taken over as usual.*

As usual? No, this was the old Dad, the one who bossed and bellowed and joked. The as-usual Dad—the one of the last eighteen months, slumped in an armchair—that Dad had gone.

'Concentrate, boy.' Dad thrust some figures under his nose. 'Mum's prepared this business plan. But we'll have to update it. With all the publicity, there's been more enquiries already. Demand's going to be stupendous—especially when the album comes out. Walenski's rainbow waistcoats will be collector's items.'

Malcolm listened as Mum and Dad argued over the

figures. No tears now, just a good old, spirited battle, just like it used to be.

'Cathy, this is a ridiculous sum for overheads.'

'No, it isn't. Here's the breakdown.'

'You've forgotten insurance.'

'Here, you're not looking in the right place. I thought we could make savings if we . . .'

Eventually they paused, satisfied, and Malcolm took a deep breath. 'There's something else,' he said. His voice came out in a rush. He'd been arguing too, inside himself, and it needed to be said while the good half was still winning.

'It's not all mine. Jeffrey should have half.'

'Jeffrey?'

'Well, yes, we were thinking of a gift, weren't we, Bob? To get his car fixed and so on.'

'I wouldn't have found it at all, if it wasn't for him. He should have half.'

'I think that's a little excessive, Malcolm.'

'It's a waste,' said Dad. 'The lad's a wally.'

'It's fair,' said Malcolm firmly.

'Well, perhaps a small proportion for his help. A fifth, no more than a quarter.'

'Half,' said Malcolm. 'Or I won't give you the business loan.'

Dad sat back red-faced. 'Don't you threaten me like that, young man.'

'It's my money.'

'I'm still your father.'

'You can't rule me.'

'I'm protecting you from yourself.'

'Jeffrey *is* family, Bob.' Mum tried to help.

'Your family,' Dad growled. 'Nothing to do with me. Nutty as a fruitcake, your cousin May. Looking at Jeffrey I'd say it's hereditary.'

'You've always had it in for them.' Mum was red-faced now. 'Ever since Grandma's ruby wedding.'

'You can't blame me for that fiasco. It was May's idea to do the catering...'

Oh dear, thought Malcolm. *Perhaps money does do funny things to people.*

'Look,' he yelled, 'if it hadn't been for Jeffrey, I'd never have made the connection. He saw Drongo near Old Harry's Seat. He recognized the waistcoat in the photo. He took me to Scotland. He worked out where the tape was. He got Scarface and Scowler caught. He...'

'He's outside,' said Mum.

A wild-eyed figure was tapping at the back windows.

Mum went to unlock the French windows. 'Come in, Jeffrey. You look like you've been through a hedge backwards.'

'Well, yes, Auntie Cathy, I have,' explained Jeffrey. 'With all those reporters outside, I thought I'd come round the back way. I went up the alley to the Sedges' garage, then climbed over their fence. You really ought to get that privet cut, Uncle Bob.'

'Hmmm. Malcolm has a suggestion,' said Dad stonily. 'I think you ought to hear it.'

'No, it was nothing,' said Jeffrey, glowing with pride as Malcolm again outlined his role in the proceedings. 'And I wouldn't dream of taking the money.'

Dad huffed and hurrumphed with relief.

'But, well, that's why I came, as it happens. I did have a suggestion about the money. It's the Adventure Centre. Big Fin sent a letter. Says they'll have to close it at Easter unless they get some more funds.'

Malcolm grinned. 'That's settled then. The Adventure Centre gets half. Shall we go and announce it to the press?'

It was a Friday in late October and Malcolm was listening to his new Walkman as he dragged his rucksack and trailed back from school. He went the long way these days—he still couldn't face the footbridge. But he hummed happily and tunelessly to himself as he planned the weekend to come, and smiled as he always did when he thought of the events of the last few weeks.

Things had quietened down now. He'd almost stopped being a local hero—but even so he wasn't quite back to plain boring Malc again.

It had been fun while it lasted. His photo everywhere—wearing one of Walenski's rainbow waistcoats, of course. He was invited to meet the Mayor, interviewed in school assembly, he even went on breakfast TV. Jeffrey came too and managed to get in a Bible verse. Malcolm kicked him and it ended with a funny yelp, but Mum said they cut that bit out anyway.

It was almost a relief to get back to normal. He could hang out in the rec. now with Razza and Marty and Si. He didn't have to worry if there was a photographer in the bushes. Giggly girls from school had almost stopped asking for his autograph. Shame really, he liked that bit. School—what a bore. But at least there was one bright spot.

Textiles.

Dad had gone round to the school and made a terrible fuss about them changing his options. Parents, honestly. He'd only put down CDT and double science because Dad insisted. 'Useful subjects, my lad. Good basis for engineering. Vital you have them.' Now Dad was insisting Malcolm did textiles and business studies instead.

That suited Malcolm—well, textiles anyway. He didn't think he'd ever make a businessman.

No matter, Dad was enough for one family. He went round in a suit these days, and carried on about cash flows and marketing plans. Actually, he didn't understand them. It was Mum who quietly sat down and fiddled at the computer and came up with the calculations. It was Mum who worked out strategies and plans and Dad who made a lot of noise and acted as if they were all his ideas. Mum just shrugged indulgently. She knew who was boss. And it was far more fun than sitting at a checkout.

So Mum set up her temporary office on the dining-room table and Dad set up Walenski's Workshop, and they were both behaving like kids at Christmas. Stacey whinged about having to do her own washing, but nobody listened.

Walenski's Workshop. Malcolm was going there now. He didn't need to, but he just liked the buzz of seeing it all happening—and Friday afternoons were special.

Down Mill Lane and right at the tortilla factory. Left at the sign that said: 'To Let—Light Industrial Units'. (Someone had scrawled in an 'i' between the 'to' and the 'let', but for once it wasn't Malcolm.) Right at the end of the units was a small sign—classy, gold on dark blue. Malcolm paused, as he always did, to read it. 'Walenski's Waistcoats. Please knock and enter.'

'Thanks, God,' he said. He did that a lot these days too. Like Big Fin said, you *could* chat to the Almighty, 'just walking around like'. And Malcolm had discovered a whacky thing—the Almighty often answered back. If you listened. Not a voice in the sky like a lottery ad, just thoughts. Ideas that popped into your head and you knew they were right. The thing was, then you had to do them.

Malcolm listened. All he heard today was the sewing machines clattering and whirring. He caught Dad's voice bellowing instructions. It was a good sound.

He stepped inside. Over the machine noise, Radio 2 was blaring. On top of that was Dad's familiar barrage: 'Take care on that pocket, Chris... Measure it, Sandy, measure it. 10.5 centimetres between button holes. Accuracy, got to have accuracy... Excellence, attention to detail—that's our motto.'

Everybody mouthed it along with him, but nobody minded. Dad's bark was worse than his bite.

Malcolm watched Percy Sedge. A gentle giant with pins in his mouth, he wielded his big scissors with the utmost care. Percy was in charge of cutting, and proud of it. He could only pump iron in the evenings these days, and Beryl had to take Maybelline for walks.

And then the big moment. A vehicle pulled up outside. Malcolm peered out. Dial-a-ride Minibus for the Disabled, he read, and saw a frail figure being lowered on the hydraulic lift. A hush fell on the workshop and a shuffle-clunking could be heard approaching. It was time for Mrs Walenski's weekly visit.

Slowly Mrs Walenski moved round the workshop, checking batches of waistcoats, stopping to look at a machine setting, inspecting the latest bales of fabric, explaining in disjointed syllables, words and mime, how to refine the latest design idea. Malcolm helped her where he could. He knew the language. There was a pause.

'Ve... Ve... Ve... Iz good stuff!' she pronounced. The workers cheered and shook her by the hand. A shrivelled, tongue-tied has-been—someone Malcolm once thought was a 'batty prune' was being treated like royalty, and the delight shone from her face.

Then Mum came in with the pay packets. Not the highest wage in the world, but they came with the immeasurable added value of a week's work well done. All these people knew what it meant to be lifted from the scrap heap.

'More orders,' announced Mum. 'Harrods are interested—and the Princess of Wales was spotted wearing a Walenski's waistcoat last week!'

On Saturdays the industrial estate was quiet. The machines were still and the radio was off. Malcolm and Dad like going there then, in the mornings, before football. Malcolm sat and pottered, listening to his Walkman, trying new stitches, thinking about new designs. Dad's purpose was more mysterious. He had got a key to the workshop next door and would disappear in there, pacing up and down, taking measurements and muttering to himself. What he was up to, he wan't saying.

Malcolm was sitting in Walenski's Workshop one sunny October morning when Jeffrey burst in.

'Have you seen it? Have you seen the papers?'

'What papers?' asked Malcolm who only ever looked at football results, cartoons and TV listings.

'Here, look.'

ROCK LEGEND IN HIMALAYAS
Ex-rock star Drongo Leadbitter is alive and well in Central Asia, according to veteran travel writer Kitty Van Melle. Drongo has not appeared in public since his disappearance eighteen months ago, and there have been fears for his safety, since rumours of his residence in Scotland proved false. But 80-year-old Kitty, recently returned from Nepal, reports meeting him by a waterfall in the remote Himalayan region of Pokhara. 'He was

*looking fit and well,' says Kitty, 'and said he was
"starting to get his head together".' He attributed his
well-being to 'meditation, hard work and fresh air' and
added that 'one day this freaky guy turned up on a
mountain and gave me a leaflet. That got me into
reading the Bible.' Drongo claimed he had not under-
gone a religious conversion, but added: 'Jesus—he said
some good stuff. Makes you think. That's what I'm
doing—thinking and seeing how the world ticks.' 'I left
him drawing water from the stream,' reports Kitty, 'and
later discovered he had joined a team of international
volunteers, working to build a health centre in the
region.'*

'How about that,' said Jeffrey triumphantly. 'Freaky
guy,' he added a little glumly.

'I think you should take it as a compliment,' said
Malcolm.

Jeffrey was definitely looking less freaky these
days. He was growing his hair a bit and talking
about getting his own flat.

He stood now, shifting self-consciously from foot to
foot, and Malcolm realized there was something he
was supposed to notice.

'Jeans, Jeffrey—you've got some jeans!'

'Bought them yesterday. Mother thinks they're terrible.'

They must be all right then, thought Malcolm.

'Look good,' he said.

'They were quite cheap,' Jeffrey continued. 'I think it
was because someone had stitched the label to the outside by mistake. Anyway, I took it off.'

Malcolm sighed a deep sigh. 'Jeffrey, that's the
most important bit.'

'The label? Why?'

'It just is.'

'Oh, well, I've still got it.' He fished it from his pocket.

'Levi's—and you took it off! Look, Jeffrey, it's meant to be like that.'

'Why?'

'It's important. It's modern culture. Just take it from me. Look, tell you what. Whip them off and I'll sew it on again. Won't take a minute.'

While Malcolm sewed, Jeffrey decided to do some press-ups.

'Need a bit of training. Sound mind and sound body and all that.'

'Huh?' Malcolm couldn't hear above the machine.

'What's your Dad doing next door?'

'What? Dunno, he goes in there a lot, talks to himself.'

'No, there's someone else there.'

'There, done. What?'

'There's someone . . . Oh, hello, Uncle Bob.'

Dad and a tall stranger stepped over Jeffrey's spindly legs quite calmly.

'This is Mr Johnson of the Enablers Foundation. Mr Johnson, this is my son Malcolm, inspiration to the venture. And, er, this is my nephew Jeffrey. Right, here's the papers I was telling you about . . .' He hustled Mr Johnson out.

By the time he returned, Jeffrey was back in his re-labelled jeans.

'I won't ask,' said Dad. 'I just won't ask.'

Jeffrey had no such inhibitions. 'What were you doing next door, Uncle Bob?'

Dad grinned and perched on the cutting table. 'I may as well tell you now . . . It's a dream—an idea I've been having—but it might just happen. Malcolm started it.'

'I did?'

'You suggested I make Mrs Walenski a chair. Well, that started me thinking about all the things that could make life easy for people like her. There're so many things. Showers, tables, chairs, remote switching devices. So I thought, once the waistcoats are up and running, why not try? The Enablers Foundation might give me a start-up donation. They'd distribute the goods. I'd start with Mrs Walenski's chair, of course. You see, all it needs is an innovative mind, engineering skills . . .'

'And attention to detail, Dad, don't forget that.'

'Trust in the Lord,' said Jeffrey solemnly, 'and he will give you the desires of your heart.'

Malcolm and Dad didn't hear, they were too busy laughing.

'I nearly forgot,' said Jeffrey after a while. 'What I really came for was to invite you. There's a PIG meeting tonight. Lovely worship band. Terrific speaker. I'm sure you'd enjoy it, Malcolm.'

Malcolm grinned. 'Sorry, not tonight, I'm afraid, Jeffrey. I've got a date.'

Malcolm and Helena sat in the back row of the cinema with their feet on the seat in front. They were munching popcorn and Malcolm's cup of happiness was full. In the gap between the tandoori restaurant ads and the coming soons, he grasped Helena's hand.

As the bored ice-cream girl came to the front, he whispered his offer.

'Helena, I wondered. You never knew, you see, but I made you a waistcoat before, you know, when . . . Well, anyway, what I thought was, I mean, can I make you a waistcoat now—a rainbow one, just for you?'

He squeezed Helena's hand and looked soulfully into her deep brown eyes.

'Oh, er, Malc...' She wriggled, embarrassed. 'The thing is, I mean, waistcoats are all right, for posh people and that. You know, for oldies. But the thing is, no one, positively no one our age is wearing them now.'

Malcolm sighed and dropped her hand. She quickly grasped his again. 'But I'd love a black Peruvian blanket coat. You couldn't make me one of those, could you?'

'Course I could,' said Malcolm, and snuggled a little closer as the lights dimmed down.